A COWGIRL'S PASSION

BARRELS AND HEARTS SERIES BOOK 3

EDITH MACKENZIE

A Cowgirl's Passion (Barrels & Hearts #3):

Images © DepositPhotos – gstockatudio & ALEX GUK BO Cover Design © Designed with Grace

Created with Vellum

❈ Created with Vellum

Lexie and Ethan, find your passion and never let it go

Gabi paced in the aisle, her frenetic nervous energy frothing inside her, bubbling to the surface. It was this very same jitteriness that kept her muscles taut as if perpetually ready for flight as she restlessly moved.

"You should sit down," Joao calmly suggested, his liquid ebony eyes glued to the giant screen as it flashed up the contestants that were next to run. "There are still five more to go till Frankie." He gave her a small, sideways smile. "Besides, Luciano will have finished his pep talk and will be out here with us before she runs."

Gabi grudgingly sat beside him, her foot twitching, sending her sable locks bouncing in time. Joao looked at the guilty limb and then back up to her face, his lips quivering as he tried to suppress his laughter.

"Don't you dare laugh at me, Joao Rojas!" she demanded, forcing her limb to be still. "I swear I don't know why Frankie was so excited you guys could make it to see her ride. It's just more aggravation, if you ask me."

"I have not seen you so nervous since you stopped wearing pigtails. It always seemed cute to me." He cast dark, laughing eyes at her. "I sometimes wish maybe you'd wear them again."

Gabi's scathing retort died on her lips when she spotted Luciano making his way to them. Jumping from her seat, she pushed past several disapproving spectators in her haste to get to him. She grabbed his arm. "Is she ready? How did she say Sampson felt? Maybe I should head back and see if she needs anything."

Luciano laughed, his eyes crinkling as he put his arm around her and forcibly returned her to her place. "How long has she been like this?" he asked the grinning Joao.

"Long enough that I worry she might cramp up from the pacing. I have tried to keep her hydrated."

Gabi let out an exasperated sigh. "Are you going to tell me how she is or not, Luciano?"

"She is focused. Sampson looks good. They are ready. Now we must do our bit and wait." He gave her an encouraging smile.

She nervously nibbled her nail, giving a start of pain when she realized she had bitten it down to the quick. Joao reached out and gently removed it from her mouth. In return, Gabi gave him an irritated glare.

"She's next." Luciano leaned forward in anticipation, his gaze intent on the arena.

Gabi edged forward in her seat, unconsciously mirroring him. Luciano was right. Even from the crowd, you could see the look of determination on Frankie's face as Sampson barreled down the chute. The girl was taking no prisoners as she guided the gleaming ebony horse around the first drum, his muscles rippling beneath his onyx hide. Horse and rider moved as one as they flew across the sand like a laser-guided missile intent on their target. The second and then third barrel were clean, Sampson chasing down the finish line like he had the devil on his heels. The time flashed up—the fastest of the day. Gabi ecstatically jumped to her feet, shrieking triumphantly.

"She did it! She just qualified for the American Rodeo!"

Joao was on his feet beside her, Gabi only vaguely aware that Luciano was also standing and cheering. Without thinking, she grabbed Joao's face between her hands and planted a great big sloppy kiss on him. Gabi jolted back to reality the moment she found herself staring into Joao's enormous, shocked eyes. Without a word, she released her hold on him and bolted from the stands, almost making as good a time as Sampson had moments earlier.

FRANKIE WAS COOLING Sampson down on a loose rein when an agitated Gabi found her out the back. "Frankie, you did it!" Gabi hollered as she approached.

Frankie slid off her horse and rushed over to her. The two girls jumped up and down excitedly as Sampson nodded his head, flapping his lips together. Frankie laughed and threw her arms around her steed. "He's such a dag, but he gave a bloody fast ride out there. I don't think he could have done any better."

"You guys were on fire. I don't think I have ever been so nervous before you've done a run. But my gosh, it was a qualifier and you did it! Can you imagine if you won the American? Since you aren't part of the top twenty riders, you would get the million-dollar bonus on top of the prize money. Today is just the best day!" Gabi beamed, doing a happy dance. Her movements stilled as she remembered having been a little too excited at Frankie's run. "Well, it would be if I hadn't accidentally kissed Joao."

"I must have too much adrenaline still in my body. For a

second there, I thought you said you kissed Joao." Frankie, giddy with triumph, slapped her knee.

"I did," Gabi admitted, the grin slipping right off Frankie's shocked face. "But in all fairness to me, it was accidental."

Frankie blinked rapidly. "I'm confused. How do you accidentally kiss someone? Where was Luc?"

"Look, I was really excited you had qualified and we were all jumping around cheering and the next minute, I was laying a big kiss on Joao."

"Huh."

"That's it?" Gabi demanded, hands on her hips. "I tell you I just accidentally kissed Joao and all you can say is 'huh'? I am very disappointed with you, Frankie."

"Oh, okay then, how about this? Your statement has left me bamboozled as to your actions and the reasoning behind them. Although, your mae will be stoked to hear the news. If Luc hasn't already called her to inform her, I will obviously relish in telling her and the girls as soon as I get an opportunity. Then we can all sit down and grill you on how you accidentally kiss a guy." Frankie finally drew a breath. "How did I do?"

"I don't want to talk about it," Gabi said, straight-faced.

"You don't want to wah?" her friend spluttered indignantly.

Taking on a dignified demeanor, Gabi waved her phone about. "I better call Bryce and give him the good news."

"That Joao finally got a kiss from you?" Frankie called out to her departing friend.

Gabi threw her friend a disgusted look. "I'm so going to increase my commission."

"I heard that."

"Good."

"What's good?" asked the voice on the phone, startling Gabi back to the present.

"Oh, hi, Bryce. Just calling to let you know the good news. Frankie has qualified for the American."

"Dang, that is good news. Y'all going to be going out and celebrating? At least have a bourbon for me."

"I think we'll have to do something tonight. While I have you on the phone, it's almost time to re-negotiate Frankie's contract, too," Gabi reminded him. "That is, if you want to still sponsor potentially the next American Rodeo champion."

Bryce laughed. "I do like your Moxy gal. Give my secretary a call and arrange a meeting."

Gabi hung up the phone, already anticipating the thrill of going into battle at the negotiation table. *Bring it on.*

CHAPTER 2

The shrill whistle of the kettle cut through the guffaws and chortles that echoed around the bunkhouse. "I guess accidents do bloody well happen." Deb threw an arm around Gabi's shoulders. "I've just never heard of accidentally kissing someone."

"I know, right? And the way she came bolting out the back to get away from him! She shot through like a Bondi tram." Frankie doubled over with laughter.

Gabi glowered at them all, her expression stony in the face of their mirth. "It's not like I meant to do it, all right?" She crossed her arms over her chest defensively. "Anyway, it was just Joao. It's not like it meant anything."

"Um, I'm not sure if you've noticed, but Joao's hot," Megan declared, fanning herself.

"So, he's not ugly." Gabi rolled her eyes in exasperation. "But I don't see him that way. I mean, I know he has a little crush on me, I'm not blind. But you know, it's Joao. He's always been around."

"Oh my gosh, Gabi. You're in denial!" shrieked Frankie, looking to her friends for support.

"Frankie's right." Deb finally walked over to pour a coffee from the cooling kettle. "Saying he has a little crush on you is like saying the Titanic is a dinghy."

"I don't even know what that is," Gabi complained. "So I'm not even sure what level of offended I should be. I'm guessing fairly?"

"A dinghy is a little aluminum fishing boat that only fits a few people if they're very close together. You mainly go up creeks with it," Megan explained.

"It doesn't even matter." Gabi shrugged her shoulders, shaking her head. "You guys don't seem to be listening to me. I. Don't. See. Him. That. Way."

"How can you not?" Megan asked, genuinely mystified. "He's hot, single, and has a thing for you."

"He's also my brother's best friend—from childhood, I might add. My father's mentoree, and the son of Papai and Mae's best friends." Gabi ticked off her list on her fingers. "He is nothing more."

"I think it sounds romantic." Frankie sighed dreamily. "And for the record, I think you protest too much."

Before Gabi could set Frankie straight, Joao, Luciano and Mitch walked into the bunkhouse. Grace was sitting high on Mitch's shoulders. Deb smiled at her husband and daughter as she walked forward. Mitch gave his wife a kiss before lowering Grace to the floor. Frankie was similarly greeting her husband, minus the child.

"You know you guys have only been apart for, like, an hour?" Megan sourly noted.

Luciano smiled knowingly at her. "One day, Megan, you will fall in love and I think I will very much enjoy watching it happen."

"Not bloody likely with the luck I have been having lately," Megan retorted.

"How was the new truck?" Deb asked her husband.

He looked down at Grace. "Did Daddy like Uncle Luciano's truck?" She nodded enthusiastically, little blonde curls bouncing energetically. "Might need to get one for myself."

Deb watched, eyes narrowed, as Gabi studiously avoided looking in Joao's direction. "Hi Joao, heard Frankie wasn't the only one that had a win at the qualifier." Gabi's eyes went wide in horror at her friend's betrayal, a burn of crimson flooding her face.

Joao smiled shyly. "It was a satisfying event."

"I bet it was." Deb winked.

"I think it's time you and Mitch find somewhere else to live," Gabi muttered under her breath.

Luciano's expression turned tragic. "You would break Sra Ana and Senhor Eduardo's heart if you took Grace away from the ranch."

"That's fine. They can leave her behind," Gabi teased.

"That reminds me. The ranch next door is for sale," Luciano said

"The old Nesbit place? The one with the river that runs through it?" Gabi's voice rose in excitement as she spoke. "I would give anything to buy that place. It would be perfect to expand the stud operations into. It has its own water supply and the soil grows good pasture. I'd just need to figure out how to raise the money."

"I have the same problem when I think about Luciano's new truck," Mitch said sympathetically. "I just bloody well need to figure out how to raise the money, too." As the group laughed at Mitch's words, Gabi noticed Joao's expression was strangely determined.

GABI ALWAYS ENJOYED A GOOD MEETING. What some people

looked at with antipathy, she relished. There was something about the thrill of back-and-forth negotiations, the friendly banter that wrapped around the steel of business. It was enough to get a girl excited. The corporate office for Black Angus was housed on one of the top floors of a skyscraper in Dallas. The interior was an eclectic mix of industrial warehouse meets Texan cowboy with polished concrete floors softened by repurposed barnwood accent walls. Exposed metal beams ran across the ceiling with elkhorn antler light fixtures. Gabi marveled at the skill the designer must have had to meld the two design styles rather than having them horrifically clash as she waited impatiently for the forthcoming battle of wills. Her palms were already sweaty on the leather laptop bag she rested on her lap.

"Gabi, I hope I didn't keep you waiting too long?" Bryce enquired as he strode forward, giving her a firm handshake before pulling her into a warm hug. "How is my favorite up-and-coming business mogul doing?"

"Primed and ready to go." She smiled. "I must get the name of your interior designer one day. Whoever it is does amazing work."

He glanced around proudly at his reception. "I will email it through. She is a talented young lady. Her work borders on art." Bryce held the door to his boardroom open. "Shall we get down to business?"

The thrill of competition sparked inside Gabi, turning her fierce. "I thought you would never ask."

"Whoa Nelly, you drive one heck of a deal. I count my blessings that you are only Frankie's manager and not Joao and Luciano's as well. You'd dang well drive me out of business if you were. I can't compete with beauty and brains,"

Bryce declared, rocking back in his high-backed leather chair. "I guess you will want to shake on it?"

Gabi batted her eyelashes at him. "What can I say? I've learned from the best."

Bryce stood and walked over to a sideboard loaded with crystal decanters and tumblers. "Can I offer you a bourbon?"

She shook her head. "Better not. I have to drive home."

He proceeded to pour himself a very generous shot before draining it and pouring another. "Good thing I only live upstairs."

Gabi looked at him in surprise. She had never given much consideration to Bryce's living arrangement. "In this building?"

"Yes, ma'am. The top three floors. The penthouse, to be precise." His eyes twinkled as he appeared to have a thought. "You could always stay over. You know, if you would like to have a drink, you wouldn't have to drive."

"Bryce!"

"I mean it strictly as a gentleman. No hanky-panky." He gave her a hopeful sideways look. "That is, unless you were thinking...?" He left the word hanging.

"Bryce Dougson. I cannot believe you are hitting on me." Gabi was shocked, though a little flattered that such an eligible bachelor was making a move on her. "You are making a move, right?"

"I was. I mean, I am. But you haven't answered the question." He stood still as a statue, waiting.

Gabi's smile was gentle. "I'm flattered. You are one heck of a catch. But my papai always said you don't poop where you eat." Bryce laughed at her words, no hint of bitterness evident. "So far, his advice hasn't led me astray. So I will have to decline and not mix business with pleasure."

His hand was warm on her back as he guided her from the room. "The man that you end up with is going to be a heck of a lucky guy." He raised her hand to his lips, his eyes lingering on hers. "But if you ever change your mind, I'll be here."

"I think that's my cue to leave." She gathered up her bag and paperwork and Bryce gallantly escorted her from the room. The click-clack of Gabi's heels echoed loudly as she headed to the elevator, a fleeting impression of loneliness from Bryce troubling her.

CHAPTER 3

The seed took root until the idea blossomed into full bloom. It niggled away at the back of Gabi's mind, forcing her into action. Finally driven to confront the thought full on, she decided to track down the one person who would be able to help her explore all options.

"Papai, would you like some lemonade?" Gabi hovered at the door, two cold drinks held in her hands, condensation running in rivulets down the glasses.

"Gabriella, it is like you read my mind." Her father blotted his face, still flushed from his exertions out in the field. "But I only need the one glass," he teased, his sun-beaten face transforming into a landscape of deep crevasses as he smiled at her.

"Very funny, Papai. You know perfectly well that one is for me." Gabi sat down on the porch swing beside him. "I just have some things running around in circles in my mind."

Senhor Eduardo pressed his lips together in mock fear. "I fear nothing good will come from that statement." A pretend shiver made his body tremble.

"Okay, are you finished being a comedian now? If I

wanted this level of humor, I could just talk to Deb." Gabi gave him a long-suffering look.

"How is my favorite adopted daughter? I have not seen her or my Grace today."

"They're fine. Now can you please focus?" Gabi snapped her fingers in an attempt to get her father's attention. "The other day, when I went and renegotiated Frankie's sponsorship contract, Bryce said something, and it really got me thinking."

Senhor Eduardo took a long sip of his drink. "What did Bryce have to say?"

"Well, a lot of things actually. But that's really another conversation and one best saved to have with the girls. The one that I want advice on is that he made a throwaway comment about being lucky I wasn't Luciano and Joao's manager as well."

"Hmm, and this got you thinking?"

Gabi took a drink of her own lemonade. "Yeah, like, I really enjoy managing Frankie and I just kinda thought it was something I would do as part of having the stud and ranch, you know?"

"But now?"

"Well, it's got me thinking."

His lips quirked. "You mentioned that."

"I mean, maybe the extra money would help with getting the ranch next door or at least make a bank think about lending me the money. And, well I think I would be really good at it." She raised her eyes to meet her father's.

"I know that since you were a little girl, you have excelled at anything you have put your mind to. But it feels like you might have a but in there," Senhor Eduardo said, seeing right to the heart of the matter. "So, why is there a but?"

"With running the business side of the ranch and all that, will I be able to handle being a sport manager as well? I don't want to be mediocre at it all. I want to be the best." An ambitious fire gleamed in her eyes, her lips pressed tightly together.

"But you do not need to run the ranch alone. You have Megan and Deb, and I think they are more than capable of stepping up and having more responsibilities than they do now. Give them a chance to prove themselves."

Gabi settled back beside her father, watching their legs slowly swing back and forth in time with the gentle sway of the swing. She turned his words over in her mind and, finding they were sound, nodded in acceptance at the truth in them.

GABI CHECKED her lipstick in her car's rearview mirror and, finding they were as immaculate as the last ten times she had looked, drew in a deep breath. Unhappy with the shakiness of it, she repeated the action, this time closing her eyes as her lungs filled to capacity, her chest rising, shoulders lifting to meet her ears. A knock on her window made her eyes fly open as she turned in alarm to confront the intruder. Frankie's grinning face peered in at her. Gabi wound the window down, the fresh air rushing in as a welcome relief to the stale air that she had been stagnating in.

"Everything okay, Gabs?"

"Yes, I was just about to get out of the car when you so rudely interrupted me."

"Oh. You know you've been sitting in your car out front of my house for the last ten minutes, right?" Frankie tried to maintain a straight face and failed miserably.

Gabi gathered up her laptop from the passenger seat and opened her door, keys in hand. "I was waiting for a song I liked to finish on the radio." She refused to meet her friend's eye.

Frankie rolled her lips together, smothering her smile as she tilted her head, brows raised, taking in her smart business attire. "Didn't hear any music when I knocked on the window."

"I'd just turned the radio off."

"Must have been a bloody long song to be out here for ten minutes."

"It was a medley."

Frankie's lips twitched. "All right then. So, are you going to come in or what? Luc and Joao are already inside waiting to find out what is so important. I must admit, I'm kinda curious myself."

Gabi made her way across the gravel drive, head held high. The effect was somewhat hampered by her unsteady progress, her heels wobbling dangerously on the uneven surface. "Not one word." She ground out to her chortling friend. It was a blessed relief to make the relatively safer surface of the porch before Frankie swung the door open and ushered her inside.

Seated at the kitchen table, Joao's eyes grew wide as saucers as he swept her appearance from top to bottom and back up again. As the shock passed, a slow, appreciative smile ghosted his lips. Setting her laptop down on the table, she smoothed her pencil skirt down before opening the device.

"I'm sure you're both curious why I asked you here today."

"It is worth it to see you in high heels," Joao said. "You should wear them more. I like how you walk in them."

"You didn't see her almost break a leg walking across the drive." Frankie laughed.

Gabi gave her friend a disgusted look for throwing her under the bus. "I have a proposition for you."

Luciano gave his friend a teasing nudge. "Settle down. It

can't be as exciting as you think since she asked for me to be here, too."

Joao gave a good-natured smile. "A man can dream."

Gabi decided the best course of action was to ignore the jibes and proceeded to hand them a printout she had prepared. Both men looked down, perusing the words before them. Frankie leaned over Luciano's shoulder, curiously reading. She looked up in surprise at Gabi.

"As you can see from that, I am suggesting that I act as your manager. I think you will find my terms fair and competitive. Frankie here"—she gestured to her friend—"can vouch for my competency. What are your thoughts?"

"Wow, Gabi, I'm shocked. I had no idea you were planning on doing this," Frankie said, looking at the men. "I mean, she has been great as a manager for me and I'm sure she would do wonders for both of you."

Luciano, expression serious, looked gravely at Joao. "Well, my friend, it is the only way she is ever going to handle your assets."

CHAPTER 4

"There are less than two weeks till the American Rodeo. I've cleared Frankie's entire schedule, so her focus between now and then will be Sampson and on keeping both of them healthy. Carlos arrives at the end of the week to wait for Delila's foal to arrive. I'll get him to check Sampson's health as well," Gabi said.

"Personally, I'm bloody looking forward to getting reacquainted with my bed. It feels like ages since I've spent more than a few days in it. A week will feel like heaven." Frankie sighed dreamily.

"And here I was thinking she was looking forward to spending quality time with us," Deb murmured to Megan.

"Speaking of quality time, Chloe flies in from Australia tomorrow to watch me ride at the American," Frankie said, clapping her hands excitedly. "I can't wait to hear how Mac's been going."

"And her timing couldn't be better. Do you think she is good enough at handling horses to pitch in while she is here? I know you said she was happy to help around the barn, but it's all hands on deck," Gabi said, bringing up the schedule for the month on her phone.

"The girl's more than capable when it comes to riding horses. If Frankie doesn't watch her back, one day Chloe could be the next big thing from Down Under." Megan picked some dirt from under her nail and gave Frankie a cheeky lopsided grin.

"Deb, have you had a chance to follow up on transferring the registration on that gray broodmare?" Gabi consulted her notes.

"All sorted, Gabi, I have everything under control. You need to stop stressing so much and let us take the load. Not just the small amount you've grudgingly handed over, but the full thing. We're all partners in this business. We want the stud to be as successful as you do."

Gabi gave the girls a remorseful little grimace, picking at the corner of her notepad. "I'm sorry. I know you guys can do it. I'm just a bit of a control freak I guess."

"A bit?" teased Megan.

"Okay, a lot then. But I don't mean anything by it." Gabi laughed. "Speaking of being a control freak, I need to wrap this meeting up and call Joao to brief him for his interview tomorrow with *Rodeo Today* magazine."

"I bet he loves it when you get all bossy," Deb said with an impish grin.

"It's strictly business, and he knows I'm doing the best for him to push his career into another gear," Gabi snapped, shuffling her papers together.

"I bet that's not all he thinks about pushing when you're around," Deb said, causing the other girls to burst out laughing. Turning a brilliant crimson, Gabi fled the room.

~

"Hello, Gabriella." Joao's voice sounded warm and intimate as he greeted her on the phone. A little tingle of something—Gabi wasn't quite sure what—flickered to life in her stomach. It wasn't an entirely unpleasant sensation.

"Hi, Joao. I just wanted to touch base with you and give you the details for tomorrow's magazine interview."

"I am glad that you called to touch my base. Do you have the details for where I am to meet them?" he asked.

Gabi wasn't sure if he'd deliberately got the phrasing wrong or if he was teasing her. These days, she found it harder and harder to tell. "I've just emailed you the details. It should be a fairly straightforward day, just be yourself. I'm sure they'll love you."

"I am not sure it is as simple as that."

"Sure it is. You'll have them eating out of your hand by the end of it," she encouraged.

"I have been myself since the day I met you and still you do not eat from my hand."

Gabi sighed. "Joao, I need you to focus. We're discussing important things right now."

"So am I," he countered.

Deciding it would be wiser not to be drawn into this line of conversation, she merely continued. "You should have received my email by now. Please let me know how tomorrow goes." And with that, she hung up. She stared at the phone in frustration. Would the man ever quit?

Gabi was in her element as the days melted away. The other girls might tease her for being bossy, but nothing filled her with more satisfaction than a well-run schedule. Taking on Luciano and Joao as clients had added another element for her to manage, and the simple truth was that she thrived on it.

The girls had ecstatically welcomed Chloe on her arrival and the slightly built girl had seamlessly slotted into life on the ranch, picking up the slack that had fallen on Deb and Megan as Gabi and Frankie's commitments had pulled them more and more away from day-to-day ranch life. Gabi was already dreading when her visit would be over and she'd return to Australia to complete her last semester of university studies. Add her brother's arrival today in preparation for the impending birth of Sampson and Delila's foal and the ranch was getting fit to burst.

Gabi glanced down at her watch. Where was Carlos anyway? Joao was supposed to have picked him up from the airport over two hours ago. Maybe she'd better give him a call to find out if everything was all right.

CARLOS GLANCED down at his vibrating phone with a wry smile and turned it over, electing to drink his beer instead. Joao gave his friend a quizzical look before his own phone began to vibrate, Gabi's name flashing on the screen. A wry smile that matched Carlos's appeared on his face as well.

"From that look, I take it my darling sister is trying to call you now, too?" Carlos speculated, spinning the beer coaster on its corner between his fingers.

"She will be wondering what has happened to you."

"What you really mean to say is she will be getting antsy that you haven't stuck to the schedule she gave you and now wants to know what is happening." Carlos stilled the coaster and narrowed his eyes. "Basically, she nags you like she is your girlfriend and wants you to do what she says, but you don't get any of the benefits. You know, like, sex?" he teased.

Joao gulped his beer as he burst out laughing. "I don't think Gabi would enjoy hearing what you are saying."

"Good thing she doesn't know where we are," Carlos countered. "You know I love you like a brother and you have my blessing for chasing Gabi, but have you really thought it over? She's my sister and I love her, but man, she's hard work. You sure you don't want a woman that is a little easier?"

Joao stared down into the amber depths of his beer mug. How could he explain what he felt for Gabi, his Gabriella? It was the very passion in her that drew him like a moth to the flames. There was a thrill to the quickness of her mind and the depths of her ambition were impossible to escape. It was like getting caught in an undertow. To him, she was quite simply everything and he would no sooner live without her than breathe. Unwilling to share his feelings even with his best friend, Joao instead elected to change the subject.

"How's your fancy girlfriend going?"

Carlos fidgeted with the button on his shirt cuff. "Evangeline? Good. I met her parents the other weekend at their Hamptons house."

"I did not know it was serious."

Joao's expression turned amused as he watched his friend tug at his collar, pulling it away from his throat. "It's early days. Her family is very different from mine. Gosh, no wonder Gabi is chasing us. Have you seen the time?" Feigning surprise as he looked down at his watch, Carlos drained the last of his beer. "We really should get a move on before she starts to worry."

Joao's eyes crinkled as a broad smirk broke out over his face. His friend raised a brow defiantly. "What?" Carlos challenged.

Joao innocently returned his glare. "I didn't say a thing."

~

"WELL, would you look what the cat dragged in?" Deb said to Gabi as the two cheery, mellow men ambled into the barn.

Gabi blew her cheeks out in annoyance. "I have been trying to get a hold of both of you for hours." She wagged a finger in Carlos's face. "I expect this kind of behavior from you." She turned to put Joao squarely in the firing line. "But you, Joao. I am disappointed."

He hung his head in shame, though his eyes twinkled. "I did not know you cared so."

"Nice touch," Carlos muttered to Megan, Chloe and Deb, where he had sought refuge.

Joao took his hat off and held it in front of his chest. "I offer you my most sincere apologies for any concern I may have caused."

"Nice," murmured Megan.

"Firstly, I was not worried, and secondly, it's common courtesy to let someone know if you are held up." Gabi ticked her complaints off on her fingers.

"I did not know you had scheduled in how long I was allowed to catch up with my best friend. And I think you care if you are nagging at me like this," Joao countered.

The gallery of spectators drew in a collective breath of awe at the cowboy's bravery in the face of danger. Gabi's face was a marvel as it contorted. Her eyes wide in shock that Joao would dare contradict her in this manner. An ugly red burned its way up from her neck until it suffused her entire face and her nostrils flared as she narrowed her eyes and flattened her lips.

"You can actually see the steam coming from her ears," Deb said. "That's not something you see every day."

"I think Mount Gabriella is about to blow," Carlos added.

"Does she do this often?" Chloe said, agog at the spectacle in front of her.

"Quite a lot when we were younger," Carlos said.

Throughout it all, Joao stood calm, as if immune to the build-up of pure rage that threatened to explode from the petite brunette across from him. Gabi opened her mouth and then closed it, her jaw working, a strange, strangled noise coming from her. Joao raised an eyebrow as he tilted his head, leaning forward as if trying to make out her words.

"I. Do. Not. Care," she ground out from between clenched teeth.

Joao leaned in even closer, his face level with hers. "I think the lady protests too much."

"The brave fool," Carlos said.

"I don't even want to watch," Megan said.

Gabi's hands clenched into fists at her side, her complexion mottling as the vein on the side of her neck popped out. "I don't care!" she shrieked and, spinning on her heels, stalked majestically from the barn.

"It will just be the two of you. If there are any signs at all that Delila will foal, I want a call," Gabi said as she mentally went over her packing checklist. "Do you think you will manage?" She looked at Carlos and Megan for reassurance.

"I'm sure I can handle him," Megan assured her confidently.

"I like a woman that knows exactly what she can handle," Carlos said, a suggestive smirk gracing his handsome face.

"Well, you'll get on fine with our Megan," Deb replied.

"You have to excuse Deb. She's laboring under the illusion that she has comedic wit." Megan glared at her friend. "But most audiences find her talents bloody lacking."

"Burn!" Deb said. "On that note, I had better go and get Grace from Sra Ana and Senhor Eduardo. You don't need me for anything else today, do you?"

"I think we are all packed. Frankie will have her gear in Luciano's truck. Everyone is meeting here at five am sharp to leave. Mitch, you, Grace, Mae and Papai will be hauling

Sampson. Frankie, Chloe, myself and Joao will be in Luciano's truck."

"Cozy." Deb wiggled her brows.

"I can shuffle it around if you don't want my parents in your truck," Gabi said.

"As if I wouldn't bloody want them in my truck. I was talking about you and Joao sitting in the backseat." Deb made kissing faces.

Gabi's expression didn't change. "Weren't you going to get your daughter?"

"On my way now."

"If it's all right, I might go with you to get Grace," Chloe said, falling into step beside Deb.

"Fine by me."

A DELIGHTED SQUEAL rang out across the yard. Underneath the Live Oak Tree, Sra Ana sat on a brightly colored blanket, the soft afternoon sun creating gentle golden puddles of light as it lazily spilled through the leafy canopy overhead. The source of the happy shriek was clinging to the back of an enthusiastically bucking Senhor Eduardo who was on all fours, her childish laughter a joy to hear.

"Did I not tell you, Sra Ana, that my Gracie is the finest bull rider in Texas?"

"You did indeed, my love." Sra Ana spotted Deb and Chloe making their way over. "I think it might be time to return this old bull back into the pasture where he belongs."

Senhor Eduardo's long face of disappointment was quickly copied by the toddler beside him. "Surely it cannot be home time yet?"

"Don't bloody look at me like that, the two of you," Deb said, stopping near them. "Gracie needs to get a good night's sleep tonight. She has a big weekend ahead of her with traveling and watching Auntie Frankie and Uncle Luciano ride."

Senhor Eduardo looked down at his pint-sized sidekick, ruffling her hair. "Maybe your mae is right. Tomorrow, we will all be going on an adventure." Grace smiled up at him before he scooped her into a giant bear hug and gave her a raspberry on her belly. Sra Ana stood and took the wriggling child from her husband to give her a cuddle and kiss.

Deb finally wrangled her child off the Cabrera's. "She's such a cutie." Chloe said, pulling funny faces to get Grace to giggle.

"She has her moments. I can tell you—she isn't so cute when she's crying for hours in the middle of the night," Deb replied, bouncing her daughter on her hip. "What have the Cabrera's been feeding you? I swear you're five pounds heavier than when I dropped you off this morning."

"If the child is hungry, we feed her," Senhor Eduardo said. "How can she be a champion bull rider if she is not strong?"

"I can hold her for a bit, if you want." Chloe held her hands out. Grace happily transferred over to the younger woman.

Sra Ana gave her an appraising look. "You're a little young, but I would say you're a natural."

"Kids have always liked me. It's why I decided to go to uni and get my degree in early childhood education. Mom reckons I should get a job working as a governess on one of those big outback cattle stations."

"What do you want to do?" Sra Ana asked.

Chloe considered the question. "I want to work with horses, but I also like kids." She shrugged. "I don't know, really. But I haven't got a job yet, so it doesn't really matter."

"You have all the time in the world to figure it out," Sra Ana said. "Now, I think we need to let Gracie go home so her mother can give her dinner." After some more blowing kisses, the women finally waved goodbye and headed back to the bunkhouse.

"I miss her already." Senhor Eduardo was glum.

"I know, my love. But I have some cookies left over from afternoon tea."

Senhor Eduardo brightened and he offered his arm to his wife. "Shall we head inside?"

Sra Ana smiled at him. "I thought you would never ask."

THE MILES FELL AWAY as the vista outside Gabi's window relentlessly rolled by. A dull ache was beginning to build inside her from forcing herself into a twisted position to stop herself from touching Joao, his broad shoulders making it next to impossible to not have body contact. She'd wanted to throttle the man when he'd settled himself in the middle space of the back seat. She could have sworn he did it deliberately too, once Frankie and Luciano had snagged the front spots.

Every part of her body was aching. She decided to give her leg a massage to help improve circulation as she maintained her rigid stare out the window at the same time. She was surprised at just how numb the limb had become. It didn't help matters that her fingertips were tingly from lack of blood from being held motionless for so long. She ran her fingers up and down her leg lightly, closing her eyes as she experimented with the pressure to see if she could feel her own touch. As feeling gradually returned to her fingers, she became aware of the hardness of her thigh muscle.

Dang Girl. All that work on the ranch is really starting to pay off. The denim of her jeans felt looser than she remembered as she trailed her fingers up and down. And then it hit her. Surely by now she should have some sort of feeling starting to return to her leg. Her eyes snapped open as she looked down in horror at her now motionless hand. A hand that rested on Joao's thigh.

"You do not need to stop. I do not know why you decided to give a massage, but I was not complaining," Joao said softly.

In the rearview mirror, she could see Luciano's shocked eyes at what was unfolding in the back seat. Snatching her hand away, she wordlessly turned her back on Joao, at least as much as her seatbelt would allow, and attempted to maintain some semblance of her dignity. From the front seat, she could have sworn she heard soft laughter.

CHAPTER 6

There was an energy in the air that Gabi hadn't been expecting. Sure, she had been to plenty of rodeos in her life, but the vibe at the American was something else. She wasn't sure what she had been expecting—maybe something like the finals in Vegas? There, it was all about seeing your heroes compete. The best of the best, toe to toe. Here, there were still the heroes. But amongst the big names were yesterday's idols that had been given one more shot at getting their names in lights or a normal person that had managed to secure their way into the line-up by beating every other hopeful for a chance to shine. The American Rodeo was the richest one-day rodeo in the world and really did have the power to make dreams come true.

Early that day, Frankie, Luciano and Joao had all taken part in the opening ceremony. Each competitor had walked from beneath the grandstand along a raised walkway lined with fireworks and cheerleaders. As they walked toward the center podium of the Colosseum, their list of achievements had been celebrated by the announcer. In the stands, Gabi's heart had swelled with pride at her friends' accomplishments, knowing the blood, sweat and tears it had taken to earn their places in the spotlight.

Living up to its name, the stadium was set up with three arenas that constantly buzzed with activity. It was no less hectic in the warmup area underneath the grandstands. Gabi wasn't sure she had ever seen so many horses trying to warm up at one time. With space at a premium, she tried to steer Sampson clear as she led him around, keeping an eye out for Frankie who was desperately trying to see Luciano's ride before her own. Sand sprayed into her face as a horse slid to a halt beside her. Gabi threw her hands up to protect herself, and Sampson snorted and pranced on the spot.

"You have got to be kidding me."

She brushed herself off angrily. Unperturbed, the culprit loped off without bothering to offer an apology. Settling Sampson down, Gabi was relieved to see Frankie making her way through the equine traffic, a beaming smile plastered on her face.

"He won!" Frankie yelled as she got closer.

"Luciano won?"

"No, he came third. Joao won." Frankie gathered Sampson's reins from Gabi's hand.

"Joao won?" Gabi asked, surprise making her features go slack.

"Yeah, let's see if I can't make it so you represent two American Rodeo champions. I need to hustle and get over to the holding pen. If you hurry, you might get to see them presenting Joao with his prizes." And with that, Frankie loped away from her shellshocked friend.

Realizing that she still stood in the warmup arena and spying the sand sprayer from before making his way toward her, Gabi gathered her wits and beat a hasty retreat to find her seat in the grandstands with the rest of the group. The prize podium was being removed from the center of one of the arenas as she excused herself past several spectators to get to her spot. Her mother, eyes shining, leaned over Deb.

"You just missed it," she accused in a loud stage whisper. "Joao won. He was so handsome standing up there proud and tall as they presented him with his check and prizes. You would have been pleased at how he carried himself."

"Why would I have been pleased?" Gabi wrinkled her nose.

"Because you are his manager, obviously," Sra Ana dismissively replied.

"You're not implying anything else?"

"If you guys are going to keep this up, I want to swap seats." Deb gave both women reproachful looks. "The barrel racers are starting, and Frankie is one of the first five to go."

Gabi gave her mother one more suspicious glance before settling back into her seat. She barely had time to get comfortable before Frankie and Sampson entered from out the back. The chute setup here was a lot shorter than the longer styles they had been running elsewhere. Picking up on the energy of the crowd, Sampson walked in short, quick steps, his head bobbing nervously with each stride. Frankie maneuvered him through the gate into the short chute, facing him away from the arena as she prepared both for their run. And then, in one smooth motion, she opened her hand and he swung around, gathering momentum in a few short strides as he launched himself into the arena.

The slender cowgirl, her fair hair flying behind like a banner on the wind, set her eager mount up for the first barrel, expertly keeping him from dropping his shoulder in too close. She urged him up and away to the second, her entire being focused on the task before her. It was awe-inspiring to watch the two of them, the girl and horse melding together seamlessly. It was hard to even remember

Sampson as the untrainable colt Senhor Eduardo had deemed too unpredictable to handle.

The last drum was clean, and Frankie asked him for more. With every muscle straining, the big black colt answered, thundering to the finish. As soon as they'd crossed, Frankie sat down heavy in the saddle and Sampson, his hindquarters sinking low, slid to a stop with mere inches between himself and the sponsorship banner at the end of the chute.

An attendant opened the gate for them to exit the arena. Adrenaline still flowing, Sampson jig-jogged his way into the holding pen and Frankie craned her neck to see their time. Once she spotted it, her eyes opened wide and she searched the crowd for her support team. Gabi quickly stood and began making her way down.

Frankie had already dismounted and had begun loosening the cinch by the time she reached her side. Luciano stood with his arm proudly around her as they waited for the times of her competitors.

"Dang girl," Gabi said. "You smoked that run."

"I know, it was like something else. I can't even explain how it felt—like the most perfect ride. He gave me everything I asked for and then some." Frankie patted Sampson's neck. "You bloody marvelous horse. You are a deadset legend." The midnight colt let out a loud snort as if graciously accepting the praise.

"Ladies and gentlemen," the announcer's voice boomed around the stadium. "The last rider of the evening is entering the arena. She's the current world champion and this year's championship race leader. She needs to beat the time of the Australian cowgirl to take the win. Need I remind you all that if she doesn't and Frankie Navarro wins as a qualifier, she earns a bonus, bringing her prize purse to one million dollars. Ladies and gentlemen, Lucy Wright."

Gabi looked to Frankie nervously, her heart beating as the anticipation built. Holding her crossed fingers out, she turned back to watch the last rider enter the ring. Lucy was riding her championship horse and it showed. The pair were clean and neat around the first two barrels, the big chestnut quick on his feet as they turned and headed for home. Gabi held her breath as the time flashed up on the scoreboard. For a moment, she was unable to process the times. Then, in a great rush, the information sunk in. Frankie had beaten the champion by 0.04 of a second.

Luciano lifted his wife triumphantly off the ground, kissing her soundly on the lips. "You did it, Querida!"

As soon as Frankie's feet touched the ground, Gabi wrapped an arm around her, jumping up and down in celebration. And then everyone was there, laughing and crying. Their faces splashed up on the big screen and Frankie was ushered away to the winner's podium.

Standing against a backdrop of American flags, her prize saddle on a stand in front of her, the event sponsors standing beside her holding the prizemoney check and buckle, she accepted the microphone.

"I used to say that winning and becoming a champion had nothing to do with luck and everything to do with hard work. But a couple of years ago, I changed my mind. Through luck, I met a family—the Cabrera's—that welcomed not only myself but my friends into their lives. I am proud to consider them my adoptive family here. They gave me an opportunity to ride their mare, Delila, and supported me when injury took her away from competition. Their daughter, Gabi, is my business partner, manager, chief cheerleader, and I am proud to say, my friend. Her vision for our stud, Infinity Ranch, has helped set my feet on the podium tonight. I also need to thank my husband, Luc"—Luciano let out a holler, the prize sponsors chuckling at his enthusiasm—"who always tells me to close my eyes and breathe when I feel myself drowning." Frankie's voice thickened with emotion. "And my friends, Deb and Megan, who believed in me enough to follow me halfway across the world on a chance. You guys bloody rock. Finally, to my major sponsor, Black Angus Western Wear, and Bryce, who is here somewhere. Winning tonight is a dream come true and is lifechanging for all of us."

"Thank you," Gabi mouthed with a sniffle, the emotion overcoming her at the validation of all her effort. Her papai pulled her in close. "I am so very proud of you and all of my girls," he murmured softly in her ear. "But then again, I always knew you would achieve great things. After all, you are my daughter."

Dabbing at her eyes, Gabi looked around at the group. She was surprised to find Joao had made his way back to them, obsidian eyes staring intently at her.

THE BAR WAS PUMPING. Inebriated patrons were yelling to be heard, the crush of people wanting to get a chance to meet the winners, especially the new millionaire winner. The mix of beer and cloying perfume mingled with the bar food as Gabi watched Luciano keeping a protective arm around Frankie at all times, steadying her on her feet when the crowd knocked her. She was impressed with how well her friend was handling the pressure, knowing how anxious she could get.

"Well, how does it feel to be the manager of not one, but two American Rodeo Champions, including one that is the talk of the town for her rapid rise to millionaire status? Not to mention another client that came third," Bryce asked, appearing at Gabi's side and offering her a drink which she gratefully accepted.

"I could ask you the same thing. How does it feel to be their sponsor?"

"Good. Or as Deb would say, bloody marvelous. I think this is my favorite win out of any competitors we have ever sponsored. This time, it feels like family has won." He drained his glass. "Another?"

Gabi looked down at her three-quarters-full drink. "I think I will be fine for a bit longer."

"Suit yourself." And with that, he disappeared into the crowd.

Seeing her parents standing with Joao on the other side of the group, she made her way over, quickly stopping at the bar, conscious of the fact she had yet to congratulate him on his win. If asked, she would have been hard pressed to find an answer as to why it had taken her so long. A surprising feeling of shyness came over her, not helped by the steady gaze Joao maintained at her approach, though he remained in constant conversation with her father. Offering up the drink she had just bought for him, she smiled winningly.

"Thought the least I could do is buy the winner a drink," she offered hesitantly, her eyes darting about as she considered if she sounded a teeny bit ungracious.

Her papai gently took hold of her mae's hand. "I think we should leave these young ones to talk."

"They must have manager-client things to discuss." Sra Ana allowed herself to be led away. Gabi shot her parents a glare at their betrayal, frantically trying to think of a reason to follow them.

"If I did not know better, I would think you have been avoiding me," Joao observed, capturing her gaze and holding it.

Gabi swallowed a mouthful of her drink, stalling. "Why would I be avoiding you? I'm your manager after all."

"I think maybe because you like me."

"I don't know if like is the right word. You're like that annoying cousin that always hangs around and won't leave."

Without breaking eye contact, he took a drink. "Are you proud of me for winning?"

"Of course. It means I'll be able to get more sponsorship deals for you and that means I get my percentage. Strictly business."

He snorted in amusement, clearly not buying her motivation. "Business, of course."

A slow burn of frustration caused her to shift her weight, her fingers drumming against her arm. "I don't like you."

Joao gave her a slow smile. "Well, I like you. Very much. And I think you like me. Very much."

The thrum of her blood pressure began to rise, her stomach tightening and hardening as her expression became pinched. Forcing herself to remain calm and her voice even, she returned his intense gaze. "I. Do. Not. Like. You." She walked away.

"If you keep running away like this all the time, Gabriella, I will begin to think you want me to chase you," he called out to her retreating back. Gabi sucked her cheeks in, swallowing the retort that sprung hotly to her lips, and resolutely kept walking.

CHAPTER 7

Laughter rang out from the bunkhouse as the girls gathered on their arrival home.

"I can't believe I know an actual bloody million-aire," Megan marveled, shaking her head in amazement. "It must have been awesome to be there."

"I'm so glad I came over to see Frankie win," Chloe agreed. "Even if it is a bit strange that I'm still too young to have a drink to celebrate with her and I've been legal back home to drink for years now."

"You have, like, a month before you turn twenty-one," Deb said. "It's not that long."

"I won't be here then. I'll be back in Australia," Chloe pointed out.

"I wouldn't bet on it," muttered Megan.

"What does that mean?" Chloe asked, baffled by her comments.

"This win. It changes everything," Gabi announced, jumping out of her chair to roam the room, frenetic energy pouring off her. "I've been thinking."

"Now, I'm bloody scared," Deb said to the room at large.

Frankie shook her head. "Nothing good has ever come from a statement like that."

"Especially from Gabi," agreed Megan. "The last time she said something like that, we all moved halfway across the world."

Gabi poked her tongue out at them. "And hasn't that turned out great?" She gathered her thoughts again. "This win has really put Frankie and our stud on the map. I'm already getting calls and emails about people sending their mares to be covered by Sampson, what youngstock we have for sale, when is Frankie available for clinics, what horses we can take for training with Frankie. That's not to mention potential sponsors for Frankie already snooping about."

"I'm already tired just listening to that." Deb pretended to take a little nap.

Frankie threw a pillow at her. "I didn't hear your name just mentioned a million times."

Gabi snapped her fingers sharply. "Focus guys." She drew in a deep breath. "So, I've been thinking that, to accommodate more visiting horses, riders, our own broodmares and youngstock, we need to look at expanding the land we have and build more facilities."

Megan looked at Gabi curiously. "You obviously have somewhere in mind."

Gabi nodded, excitement coursing through her body. In her mind's eye, she could already see the horses grazing beside the river, the extra barns and arenas that would be built. "The Nesbit place."

Contemplative silence greeted her announcement. "It's worth a bit isn't it?" Megan tentatively asked.

"It is, but…" Gabi looked appealingly to Frankie.

Frankie laughed. "But you know someone who has

recently come into a bit of money and also happens to be a part owner in the stud."

"Something like that," Gabi admitted. "But it would be a sound investment."

Frankie spread her hands wide. "I didn't say no."

"Is that a yes then?" Gabi dared to ask.

"I think I need to talk to Luc first. It's a pretty big decision without at least going through the motions of discussing it with my husband."

"Thank you, Frankie."

"In the meantime, it couldn't hurt to at least call the realtor and enquire, right?"

"You don't have to tell me twice." Gabi almost broke a nail in her haste to dig her phone out of her pocket and rapidly started dialing the number. She held her breath as the line rang, nerves slapping into her as the receptionist answered. "Hello, I am calling about the Nesbit Ranch that you have for sale."

"I'm sorry, the owners accepted an offer for it yesterday."

Gabi pressed a trembling hand to her temple, her heart sinking at her words. "What do you mean they accepted an offer?"

"The property sold yesterday. I'm very sorry."

Gabi quietly thanked the receptionist and hung up the phone, suddenly feeling bereft. "It's been sold," she muttered without looking at any of her friends.

She rushed from the room and didn't stop running until she reached the fence of the broodmares paddock. Disappointment settled over her like a cloak as the realization that the vision she had seen in her mind would never eventuate. Hot tears trickled down her face. In the background, she could hear the gentle swish of horses' tails as they swatted flies away.

"It really meant that much to you, hey?" Frankie appeared beside her distraught friend.

Gabi swiped at her tears with the back of her hand. Sniffing, she nodded, her bottom lip trembling. "It really did. It really does."

"Well, I just spoke to Luc, and it doesn't help with buying the ranch, but he agrees that we should invest the money into the stud one way or another."

"Really?" Grateful tears replaced the earlier disappointed ones. "That's amazing. And I know I did my whole investment spiel back in there, but it's also incredibly generous of you both."

"I remember a woman who took a chance on a scared, anxious cowgirl from Down Under. Luc remembers all that your family did for him. You believed in us, and we believe in you and your vision for this stud."

"You're going to make me cry even more," wailed Gabi.

"You're going to get me started," Frankie cried, fanning her face. "Now you just need to sit down and figure out what the next step for the ranch is."

GABI LOOKED down at her ringing phone and rolled her eyes in frustration as she silenced the call. "Joao again?" Frankie asked.

"Yeah. He's left a few messages now and I have told him that I am busy. He's just going to have to wait till I'm free this afternoon."

"Does she treat you like that?" Chloe said.

"No, why would she?" Frankie asked.

"Well, she's your manager too," Chloe stubbornly pressed.

"I think what you're missing here is the fact it's the guy that has the hots for her," Deb said.

"Right, I forgot about that," admitted the younger girl.

"How can you forget about that?" questioned Megan. "The guy practically follows her around like a puppy. I'm beginning to think she likes it or, should I say, she likes him?"

"I don't like him," Gabi said, lacking her usual conviction. "Now, if we have finished discussing Joao, can we get back to what I was saying? Good. You all know how upset I was about not being able to extend the land that our stud currently resides on. After much careful consideration, I think the best investment of funds would be to build and outfit a purpose-built veterinary barn, complete with an operating theater, crush, lab, ultrasound machine and living quarters. I'm thinking we should also build sick bays and yards. Thoughts?"

Deb mulled it over. "I like it, everything can be done in-house now. It will save a lot of time with hauling mares over to the vets every time we need a scan or something."

"We can use it as a big marketing advantage for visiting mares as well," Megan added.

Gabi looked hesitantly over to Frankie. "As the one with all the money, what do you think?"

"It would have bloody come in handy when Delila got hurt," Frankie said.

Gabi raised her eyebrows in question. "So is that a yes?"

Frankie broke out in a broad grin. "I like the idea. It's a bloody yes from me."

Gabi leapt from her chair and threw her arms around the girls. "Thank you so much. You wait and see—this is the beginning of something big."

SCANNING THE BUSTLING DINER, Gabi located Joao in a booth nestled against smudged windows and overlooking the parking lot. Sidestepping several waitresses, she made her way over.

"Okay, you can stop blowing up my phone, I'm here." The vinyl of her seat creaked as she shifted her weight to open her leather-bound folder and withdrew a sheath of papers. "As you can see, you are one very popular man right now." Joao averted his eyes as their gazes met, making Gabi pause her diatribe. "I would have thought you would be more pleased by the news. Isn't that why you have been hassling me since yesterday?"

Joao rubbed the bridge of his nose. "I need to tell you something. Something I did."

"Please tell me you didn't agree to deals. Not without letting me go over them first. They will try to take advantage of you. Just tell them to talk to me and I will handle it all." She shook the papers in her hand at him. "And I think you will be pretty happy with what I have in here."

"I'm the one that bought the ranch."

Gabi blinked rapidly, her face going slack. A feeling of cold cascaded over her, an unsettling heaviness in her chest. Suddenly, the noise of cutlery clinking on tables and scraping against plates and the hubbub of conversation were all too loud. "What do you mean?"

"The Nesbit place. I'm the one that bought it, but I can explain why," he rushed on.

Gabi slowly stood, openly staring at him with a pained look of hurt and anger. "I don't think I need to hear anything more from you. You knew how much I wanted that place. I thought we were friends." She swallowed. "How could you do that to me?"

"Gabriella, if you will just listen, I can explain," he pleaded, reaching out for her across the table.

Gabi recoiled. "We have a contract and I understand that I still have to be your manager, but from now on, it's strictly business. So, here are your offers. You can read them your-self." She threw the papers in his face and dashed from the diner.

Once in the safety of her car, she sobbed, pounding on her steering wheel in anguish at his unexpected betrayal.

CHAPTER 8

$\mathcal{L}$ong spindly legs splayed out awkwardly, threatening at any moment to collapse and fold under the foal, her body quivering with the supreme effort of remaining upright. Delila gently nuzzled her, encouraging her around to her full udder. Shakily, one tentative step at a time, the foal made it to her destination and, guided by instinct, followed the smell of her dam's milk. Latching on, her little fuzzy brushtail pumped in rhythm with each suck. The friends hung over the door of the stall, awestruck at the miraculous sight of new life. Pieces of straw still stuck to the filly's damp coat as she lifted her head, her muzzle milky from her drink, and surveyed the group that observed her.

"I think we might have another buckskin on our hands," Megan noted in a hushed tone.

"A little Delila," agreed Frankie, not taking her eyes off the foal that represented the hopes for the future of the ranch.

"On that note, what should we call her?" asked Deb, looking at Gabi.

"I've been thinking about that. What do you guys think

about Nova as a name? Because she is going to be our bright, shining star."

Frankie contemplated the foal in front of her, laughing gently as the baby animal lost its balance and fell into the deep straw, a tangle of limbs. "Well I think our bright star needs to learn a few things first before we put that pressure on her. But I like it."

Gabi pushed herself off the stall door. "We should let mother and daughter bond," she whispered. "Anyway, there are a few things we need to discuss."

"She's calling another bloody meeting, isn't she?" grumbled Deb.

"Looks like it," Megan said, giving Chloe a sour look when she started giggling at their complaining. "I don't know why you think this is so bloody funny. No one escapes these things without a to-do list a mile long."

"But I'm leaving at the end of the week. How much could she possibly give me?" Chloe said as they strolled back to the bunkhouse.

"You'd be surprised," Frankie said, holding the door open for the others to enter. "Our Gabi doesn't believe in placing restrictions on herself."

Gabi was already busily typing away on her laptop by the time the girls settled themselves into their usual places. Her fingers flew across the keyboard, giving rise to little tapping noises. Noticing her friends were ready, she clicked on a few final keys and closed the screen. "The emails have been going crazy since you won, Frankie. It's almost a full-time job just keeping up with that."

"What can I say? When you're hot, you're hot." Frankie winked at her friends.

"Well, you are definitely hot right now and we need to capitalize on it. Firstly, there's a lot of interest for mares to be sent to Sampson to be serviced. We need to start getting plans drawn up for the vet facilities and move that along as fast as possible. Till then, Megan and Deb, you are going to be spending a lot of time hauling horses to be scanned at the vets."

"How many of us are there again?" Megan whined, shaking her head at Deb.

"Enough to get the job done for now," Gabi continued. "I think it's best if we concentrate on only training the horses we have bred and current clients and close our books to all others."

"That's still a lot of bloody horses to work a day, especially as I will be helping Deb with the extra hauling and care of more visiting mares," Megan said.

"That's where I was hoping Chloe could help," Gabi said, looking at the young Aussie.

"Sure, I'm happy to help anyway I can, but I'm not sure how much I will be able to do for the week I have left," Chloe said.

Gabi gave her a winning smile. "Well, I was hoping maybe after you finish up your course at University, you might consider coming back and working here? We would love to have you."

Chloe looked shellshocked. "I, um, you really want me here?"

Frankie clapped the younger girl on the back. "I couldn't think of someone I would like to have here working with us more. In all fairness, we have been promising Megan more help for a while now."

"It's been over a year," Megan grumbled.

Gabi stared intently at Chloe. "So, what do you think?"

Chloe's face split into a broad grin. "I'd love to. I mean, I have a semester left and I would have to sort Mac out and, well, stuff. Wow. This is really happening."

Gabi gave a relieved sigh. "I'm glad you agree. I didn't

really have a plan B on that one. Now, I am getting lots of enquiries for people that want to train with Frankie as well and that one is going to be a bit harder to manage."

"I'm hardly ever home as it is," Frankie said, her mouth thinning as she looked doubtfully at the Brazilian girl. "How would I manage to fit any sort of consistent training in for people?"

Gabi scratched at her arm in thought, "I've been thinking about that, and as far as I can decide, I think we should offer a few set dates a year for clinics. Hire a venue or figure out a way to have them here. You could do some demonstrations on how you train your horses, and maybe Deb and Megan could show the routines we have for our top-level horses and then give them a few one-on-one lessons."

"I still think I am going to be spread pretty thin, but it at least sounds doable."

"Excellent, well that was all I really wanted to cover," Gabi concluded.

"Oh, no, you don't," Deb interrupted.

"Don't what?" Gabi scrunched her face up at Deb's tone.

"So, we really aren't going to talk about the bloody elephant in the room then?"

"She means Joao," Megan said, nodding in agreement. "And I think she's right."

Frankie groaned. "Don't say that."

Gabi smiled at Frankie, grateful for her support. "Thank you, Frankie, I agree. It's not something we need to discuss."

"Oh, I think we definitely need to discuss it," Frankie said, surprising Gabi. "I meant Megan telling Deb she was right. We don't need that kind of energy around here. You know what she will be like after being told that. She's bloody difficult at the best of times, but that sort of talk will make her nearly impossible to deal with."

"Fine." Gabi crossed her arms over her chest and leaned

back in her chair. "There isn't anything to talk about. Joao knew I wanted to buy that ranch and he went ahead and snatched it straight out from under my nose—all our noses, if we want to be honest with ourselves. That's not the action of a friend."

Frankie took a steeling breath, looking around the table for support. "Luc says he is taking it badly."

"Good," exploded Gabi, slapping both hands on the table and making everyone jump at the sharp noise. "He deserves it."

Frankie raised her eyes to meet her friend's. "You don't know that. Have you bothered to find out why he did it?" At Gabi's continued silence, she pressed her advantage. "You once told me that I needed to give Luc a chance to explain his side of things and, if I hadn't, I would have thrown everything away on a misunderstanding."

"This is different."

"How?"

"First of all, you and Luciano were in love. Secondly, there is nothing Joao could say that would make me forgive him," Gabi declared hotly, her mouth thinning.

Chloe looked like she wanted to be anywhere else but in this room at this precise moment. Deb stared down at her hands and Megan's gaze kept flicking toward the door as if plotting her escape. But Frankie's gaze remained unwavering.

"I think you owe it to yourself and him to at least hear him out. You can't give him the cold shoulder forever."

Gabi's jaw jutted out mutinously. "Watch me."

GABI HELD HER HAND UP, stopping her approaching brother dead in his tracks. "Don't even."

"What?" he asked innocently.

Around her, she could hear the birds chirping merrily, joyous in the beauty of the day. The air was already warming up, making Gabi thankful that she had chosen to escape her friend's grilling by hiding out on the patio.

"I don't want to talk about Joao. Mae has already expressed her disappointment at my handling of the situation and the girls have thrown in their opinions. I don't need you nagging at me too. I've had it up to here with everyone telling me what to do. I am not going to change my mind, end of discussion"

Her brother lowered his lanky form into the chair beside her and helped himself to a cookie from the plate in front of her. "Mae can't be too upset if she still fed you."

"She's trying to sweeten me up."

"You're being stupid, you know," he said as he took a bite, crumbs falling from his mouth as he spoke.

Gabi stuck her fingers in her ears and began to sing loudly, drowning out Carlos's voice.

"Real mature, Gabi." He reached over, attempting to pull her hands away. After a short tussle, he was successful and returned to eating his cookie. "That's not why I want to talk to you, anyway."

She gave him a dirty look. "Maybe you should have started with that, then."

Perhaps it was the edge of maturity of those few extra years he had on his sister or maybe it was the benefit of long years of dealing with Gabi's moodiness, but he wisely chose to ignore her. "I think it would be a waste spending all of that money on the vet complex and only have it used by a visiting consultant." He held his hand up for silence, unconsciously mirroring his sister's earlier gesture. "I'm not saying the complex isn't a good idea, just that it could be utilized better. I would like to offer you a proposal."

Gabi bit down ferociously on the cookie in her hand. "Go on, I'm listening."

"I would like to lease the facilities off you and base myself out of there running an equine vet clinic." Stalling any objections, he rushed on. "Obviously, Infinity Ranch horses would have priority at the practice, and you get the added benefit of having a vet onsite at all times."

"Mae and Papai would be pleased to have you home permanently again."

"What about my kid sister?" he asked giving her a goofy smile.

"The jury is still out on that one. But I think it makes sense from a business point of view. I will get the lawyer to draft something up for you to sign."

"Hey, I'm your brother," he protested giving her a shocked look that hardened into disbelief.

She leaned forward and gently patted Carlos on the cheek. "And this is just business. Nothing personal."

CHAPTER 9

*T*he foal frisked about the small paddock, bucking into the air on spring-loaded legs. Oblivious to the young one's joy below him, an eagle flew overhead, letting out a cry as he scouted for food. The smell of the sun-warmed earth rose up with each step that Gabi took as she and Frankie escorted their guests of honor toward Nova and her dam.

"Thank you for letting us come and meet the foal. I didn't think Teeny could have gotten any more excited if I told her we were going to Disneyland," the tall man said to Frankie, keeping a firm hand on his daughter as she skipped beside him.

Frankie gave an easy laugh as she tousled the little girl's hair. "Wow, more exciting than Mickey Mouse. I'll take that."

"Daddy, Daddy," whispered Teeny in an awestruck voice as she tugged on her father's hand. "I can see them. I can see Delila and the baby."

Gabi smiled at the excitement in the child's voice. With how tense it had been around the ranch the last few weeks, it was nice to watch the joy and simple pleasure a horse could bring. She swung the gate open.

"If you like, Travis, you and Teeny can go in and meet Nova up close and personal."

Teeny's eyes went saucer wide as she looked up pleadingly at her dad. "Please, Daddy, can we go in?"

Frankie pulled out some sugar lumps from her pocket. "It just so happens that I have some of Delila's favorite treats in the whole wide world. Maybe you might be able to help me give them to her?" Without hesitation, Teeny linked hands with her and walked over to the buckskin mare.

"I never imagined the famous Frankie Navarro would actually make good on her promise way back when," Travis admitted to Gabi as they leaned on the gate, watching his daughter feed the mare. Curious about all the attention, Nova tentatively stretched out a whiskered muzzle to sniff at the newcomer. Teeny giggled as the hair tickled her hand. "You people are good folks. I try hard to make sure she is happy, but it's been hard since we lost her mother to cancer. Most of the time it's just her and me. I swear she spends more time with the bulls than humans most days."

Gabi's face softened as she glanced at him, the look rich with acknowledgement of his pain and worry for his little girl. "I'm very sorry to hear about your wife, but from what I can see, you have a happy, well-adjusted little girl there. And for what it's worth, the one thing you can always count on with Frankie, if she gives her word, she means it. Teeny made quite the impression on her that year she met her at Cowboy Christmas." Out in the field, Frankie swung Teeny up onto Delila's back, the child's grin splitting her face in two.

Afterwards, the group ambled into the coolness of the barn. Chloe popped her head out of the stall she was cleaning. "Deb has gone to have morning tea at the Cabrera's with Grace, and Megan has popped into town to grab something," she said by way of greeting. Teeny let go of her father's hand and waved at her. "Hi cutie, what's your name?" Chloe asked.

"My name is Catrina Decker, but no one except my great aunt Thelma calls me that. Mostly I just get called Teeny 'cause I'm so small."

Chloe smiled indulgently at the flurry of words that flowed from the small visitor's mouth. "Well, my name is Chloe, and I was just about to go upstairs and get myself a snack. Are you hungry at all?"

Travis laughed heartily. "She was born hungry. For such a small package, I don't know where she puts it all."

"Well, it's a good thing. Because we were having such special guests come to the ranch today, Frankie brought some of her ooey gooey chocolate brownies over. Do you think you might like some?"

Teeny's face dropped in disappointment, her bottom lip jutting out. "I don't know if I am allowed to have brownies that you are saving for your special guests."

Chloe smiled at her gently. "Honey, you and your dad are the special guests."

Teeny's face lit up with pleasure. "Really?"

"Yep, really."

Frankie laughed. "I think that's a yes." Not needing another word of encouragement, Teeny followed Chloe as she led the way for the group up into the bunkhouse.

GABI ALMOST STUMBLED over the suitcases lined up near the door. "Are you sure you arrived with this much stuff?" she asked Chloe in amazement.

"I'm actually going home with an extra suitcase. The extra baggage charge is going to be a killer." Chloe laughed. "But you guys have the best boots over here. Don't tell Mom I spent all of my pay on them."

Gabi thought it felt deeply wrong that the young Aussie girl was leaving for home. Rationally, she knew that she would return in a few short months and this time for good, but for now, she was going to miss her a great deal more than she had anticipated when she had arrived only a couple of months earlier.

"Give your mom a hug for me," Frankie said. "And make sure she sends me lots of Mac updates, especially when she starts doing her first rodeos. She's going to have a blast with him."

"Have you got everything, kiddo?" asked Deb, looking at the suitcases. "You haven't forgotten anything?"

"Looking at the mountain of baggage she has piled up, do you think it looks like she has forgotten anything?" Megan said. "I swear some days it's like I'm the only one that has common sense around here."

Chloe looked at the bickering pair fondly. "I'm going to miss you guys." She opened her arms wide for a group hug. "All of you."

Gabi sniffled. "Make sure you hurry back to us, okay?"

"Don't you start crying! You know it gets me started," wailed Frankie, clutching everyone close.

"Okay, enough of this," Deb said, letting go to gather up a suitcase in each hand. "Everyone, grab a bag and let's get this show on the road."

CHAPTER 10

Gabi wheeled her overnight bag behind her, silently cursing her delayed flight that meant she now had no time to check her luggage into her hotel and instead had to hotfoot it directly to the rodeo venue. She mentally added it as another reason why Joao was causing her more trouble than the backstabber was worth. Ahead, she could make out the traitor, scanning the grounds to try to locate the cause of whoever was staring an angry hole right through him. Spotting her scowling face, he smiled and hurried over, trying to take the bag from her hand. Gabi stubbornly tightened her grip, refusing to relinquish it into his care, and raised narrow eyes to his, daring him to escalate the situation into an outright wrestle for control. Joao's nostril's flared, his mouth downturned.

"I hoped you had calmed down by now," he said, blocking her path.

"I am perfectly calm," she icily replied. "Another thing I am is a complete professional. I am here tonight in my role as your manager and to meet with the representative from

Ironside Protection that are interested in sponsoring you." She neatly sidestepped him.

"Gabi, if you would just listen, I do not think you would be so mad," he said, jamming the wheel of her suitcase with his foot, abruptly halting her forward progress.

"I have said all I need to say. I will represent you to the best of my ability here tonight, but there is no need for us to have any discussions outside of business." She attempted to tug her bag free.

Joao's lips pinched together and his posture stiffened. Cursing under his breath, he moved his foot, releasing her precious luggage and sending her flying in the process. "You are being a stubborn little fool who needs to swallow her pride before it chokes her and listen to someone else for once."

"It will be a very cold day in you-know-where, before I listen to another word you have to say," Gabi cried, straightening herself and once again battling the hurt that his betrayal caused her. "In fact, I don't even want to be anywhere near you, let alone hear what comes out of your mouth."

Joao's hands balled into fists at his side, the muscle in his jaw bulging as his jaw clenched. His usually gentle, liquid eyes turned molten with rage. "You should know that I had my reason to do what I did, and it had nothing to do with hurting you. In fact, it was the complete opposite. But I'm done, Gabriella. After this rodeo, you can consider our management contract null and void. I release you. You got your wish. You won't have to have anything to do with me ever again," he sneered, storming away from her.

Eyes burning with humiliation, Gabi's breath hitched in her chest at the sight of his departing back, a crawling sensation of … loss … shivered up her spine. She shook her head to dispel that notion. She was happy, elated even, to not have to deal with that jerk anymore. Adjusting her grip on the handle of her bag, she headed down the walkway, looking for a restroom to freshen up before she met with the potential sponsors.

~

SMOOTHING DOWN HER SHIRT, she gave a quick cursory glance down at her shoes to make sure she wasn't trailing any dreaded toilet paper. Deciding she had made herself as presentable as possible given the circumstances, she opened the door and headed up toward the corporate boxes.

"Gabi!" an excited high-pitched voice called a second before what felt like a small calf hurdled straight into her side, knocking the wind out of her lungs as they fell to the ground in a tangled heap. Stars danced in front of Gabi's eyes as she desperately tried to suck in a breath.

"I'm so sorry, Gabi," a deep, masculine voice apologized somewhere above her. "Teeny, you need to say sorry. I think you might have actually broken Gabi." It took a moment for the words to penetrate her dazed mind and she gladly accepted the hand that Travis offered, allowing him to help her to her feet and brush her off.

"I'm sorry, Gabi. I was just so happy to see you," Teeny said, staring down at her feet.

Gabi wrapped an arm around the girl. "And I am so happy to see you, too." She looked up at Travis. "Are you guys here competing or spectating?"

"Neither. I'm supplying some of the bulls for tonight," he replied, handing Gabi's suitcase to her after inspecting it for damage.

"Yep. Daddy breeds some of the nastiest bulls this side of … well, everyone says that they are feral. But Buttercup and

Wonky Donkey are always nice to me," Teeny said, taking Gabi's hand.

"Ah, Buttercup and Wonky Donkey?" Gabi raised her eyebrows at Travis, her generous mouth twitching.

"I should have known better than to let this one name all the bulls we breed." Travis sheepishly ruffled Teeny's hair. "Would you care to join us?"

"Any other time, I would jump at your invitation, but I have to meet with some sponsors for a client tonight. Maybe I can take a raincheck?" she asked, giving Teeny a hug.

"Sure thing, Gabi," Teeny said, grabbing her father's hand. "Bye." She waved enthusiastically as the pair walked off. Gabi waved until they disappeared around the corner and, once again, attempted to make her way to her meet and greet with the Ironside Reps.

THE CORPORATE BOX was filled with a mixed crowd in what could only be described as corporate cowboys. Gabi was confident that some of the boots in the room had never been on anything dirtier than a boardroom floor. The odors wafting from the bain-maries made her stomach rumble. From seats in front of the floor-to-ceiling glass windows, Butch Hendrikson waved her over. Dodging scurrying hostesses, Gabi made her way toward him, marveling at how removed she felt this far away from the action. It was surreal, like looking down on little dolls.

Butch stood and extended his hand in greeting. Gabi noted his firm grip with approval. "Miss Cabrera, it is a pleasure to finally meet you in person. I've been a fan of your father's for years." The sandy-blond man beside him eyed her openly, his gaze astute. "This is our head of marketing and promotion, Taylor Pearson."

"Pleasure, Miss Cabrera." Taylor gestured to the spot beside theirs. "Please, take a seat."

Lowering herself into the red leather chair, Gabi smiled at them warmly. "Butch, Taylor, please call me Gabi. And thank you for meeting with me like this." She looked at the vista below. "Quite a view from up here."

"It is, but if you ask me, we're too far from the action. You want to feel the sand hitting the side of the arena," Butch said.

"How is your man, Joao, feeling about the bull he has drawn for tonight?" asked Taylor, accepting a drink from a hostess. "Can I get you something?"

"A beer would be great," she replied, smiling her appreciation. "He was fired up when I spoke to him on my way here."

"That's good to hear," Butch said, jovially. "A bull rider needs to have a bit of fire in his belly." Below, the lights dimmed, the announcer's voice building the anticipation of the event that was about to start.

"Well, he was certainly feeling something." Gabi took her drink from the hostess and smiled her thanks. Fireworks reflected off the glass panel as the competitors were announced, stepping through a ring of fire one by one.

"He looks like he means business," Taylor said, peering down below where Joao stood beside Luciano, proudly staring out at the crowd as the announcer called for everyone to stand for the American Anthem.

Gabi stood tall, unconsciously matching Joao's posture as the opening refrain of the Star Spangled Banner filled the stadium. Her mind drifted to his parting words. Surely he didn't mean that? She would secure this deal and present it to him, and if he still felt that way, then fine. It was his loss. She was one heck of a manager. The last chords of the anthem rang out. Satisfied with her plan of attack, she turned to the men at her side.

"Speaking of business, isn't it time we discuss your proposal?"

~

"I CAN SEE why you exclusively represent some of the best professional rodeo athletes in the sport," Taylor said, leaning back in his chair. A respectful expression replaced what Gabi had begun to suspect was his poker face.

"Just trying to keep my clients happy," Gabi modestly replied. *Not that Joao appreciates it.*

Butch leaned forward. "Looks like Joao is getting ready now. It's one heck of a matchup. Widow Maker has bucked every cowboy off in his last twenty outings."

"My man is up for the challenge," Gabi asserted confidently.

She shifted in her seat, watching as Joao readied himself on the side of the chute, a restless Widow Maker eager for the upcoming battle. Joao gingerly lowered himself on the bull's broad back, Luciano holding him steady as the beast plunged beneath him, resenting the cowboy's weight. Wrapping the rope around his gloved fist, he reached out his free hand to grasp the chute rail, his face steely with resolve. The movement of his head was quick and certain as he nodded for the gate to open.

The great bovine surged from his confinement, great ropes of spittle trailing from his gaping mouth. Joao sat balanced, his weight centered, as Widow Maker whipped around to the left, his hind legs kicking high as he corkscrewed, sinew and hide twisting, the muscles corded. Gabi's steepled hands were sweaty. Inching forward, she barely breathed, willing the clock to count down.

"Dang, I think he's going to be the one to finally ride him." Butch hollered, raising to his feet in anticipation.

The wily bull, not willing to give in, suddenly switched direction, the change in velocity causing Joao's weight to shift. Uneven from the bovine's pivoting hooves, the sand underneath caused Widow Maker to stumble, toppling the unexpecting cowboy forward. Attempting to right himself, the bull flung his great head back. Joao's head slammed into the beast's skull, his body going slack.

"No!" Gabi screamed, desperately grasping the armrest, half pushing herself jerkily to her feet. In slow motion, the drama unfolded before her stricken eyes, every detail painful to watch. The unconscious cowboy, strung up by his rope, dangled like a limp doll off the side of the now berserk bull.

"No, no, no." She let out a long, anguished cry of denial at the events happening before her.

The rodeo clowns worked as a team, diving in to distract Widow Maker, tapping him on the head whilst others threw their weight on him, urgently trying to undo the buck strap to stop the bull's plunging. Miraculously, Joao's hand slid free from its entanglement, his boneless body crumpling in a heap in the sand. Having been goaded beyond his endurance, the bovine charged after the clowns and out into a laneway.

Gabi, a bloodless fist pressed to her mouth, watched ashen-faced as the rodeo clowns huddled around his body, urgently signaling for medical assistance. Luciano desperately jumped off the chute rails, sprinting to his prone friend. Blood pounding in her ears, Gabi brushed off restraining hands, her legs propelling her from the room, her only conscious thought to get to Joao's side.

CHAPTER 11

A shaven-haired security guard stepped into Gabi's path, halting her frantic dash. "Ma'am, this is for competitors and officials only."

Gabi vehemently shook her head, dark locks, damp with perspiration, wildly flying. "You don't understand, I have to get to Joao."

"I don't know who Joao is, but without a pass, you can't get back here." Her tormentor folded thick arms across his burly chest.

"I have a pass. Not here, it must be with my luggage." Her breath came out raggedly as she tried to make herself understood, fear causing rational thought to flee. "I need to get to Joao. Please, just let me through."

"I can't do that, Ma'am." Immovable as a boulder, the guard maintained his ground.

"Please," sobbed Gabi, breaking down. "I need to be there."

"Gabi?" Luciano's voice sounded from behind the guard. "Why are you not already with Joao?"

She pointed to the security. "He won't let me pass. Luciano, I need to see him."

Luciano reached around the guard and grabbed Gabi's arm. "She is coming through. If you don't like it, talk to my manager." Pushing past the man, the pair rushed down the corridor. "You must be quick. They already have him with the paramedics."

Rounding the corner, they were confronted with a huddle of medical personnel around a prone form strapped to an orange spinal board, oxygen mask over his face. Gabi's legs began to give way as she hyperventilated. Luciano propped her up, lowering his face until they were eye to eye.

"Gabi, now you must be strong. Breathe. He is going to need you."

Gabi nodded, fear making her mute. She grimly made her way through the press of people, Luciano stoic by her side. "I am his manager. What is his condition?"

A lanky paramedic with a startling shock of silver hair glanced up at her before returning to monitoring Joao. "He's unresponsive. We are about to move him into the ambulance for transfer to emergency. Will you be traveling with him?"

Gabi answered without hesitation. "Yes."

The paramedic nodded. "On the count of three, lift. One. Two. Three." Gabi quickly jumped into the back of the ambulance, meeting Luciano's anxious gaze as the doors closed and the vehicle pulled away, sirens blaring. "I'm Officer Steele." He smiled reassuringly at her and nodded to his red-headed companion. "And this is Officer Thompson. We are going to do our very best to get this man safe and sound to hospital. Does he have any medical conditions that we need to know about?" he asked, rummaging in drawers and opening packaging.

"No," Gabi replied in a shaky voice, a cold feeling expanding into her very core.

"Excellent." Officer Steele waited whilst Officer Thompson cut Joao's shirt open, revealing a surprisingly smooth chest. He placed two electrodes on the cowboy's chest and another two lower on his abdomen. The cords attached to a monitor. "This machine is an ECG. We use it to monitor heart rate," he explained soothingly.

Gabi hugged herself tightly, fearful eyes following their every movement. Suddenly, the monitor began to beep, the lines changing. Joao's complexion turned waxy, a pallor to his normally swarthy skin. The paramedics leapt into action, pulling the oxygen mask off his face and beginning to perform CPR. Gabi felt dizzy, the world beginning to fade to gray. She closed her eyes tightly, too scared to watch.

"Breathe," she whispered. "Please, Joao, breathe." She could hear the monitor continue to beep. "Get the defibrillator," instructed Officer Steele. Rustling sounded as Gabi bit down hard on her lip, the taste of blood filling her mouth. "And clear." A low thud. Silence. The wail of the sirens melted away. "And clear." Silence. And then the most beautiful sound she had ever heard—a steady rhythmic beat on the ECG. "It's okay, you can open your eyes," encouraged Officer Thompson. "He gave us a bit of a scare, but we have stabilized him for now." Gabi opened her eyes, tears spilling from them as tremors rocked her body, her gaze fixated on Joao's unmoving form.

THE BATTERED PLASTIC doors flapped shut, blocking her from following Joao's stretcher into the emergency room. Gabi stood stock still, drained. "Are you gonna move or what?" a harsh voice asked.

Uncertain what she should do next, she shuffled to a vacant beat-up chair beside a man that held a blood-stained cloth to his hand. Everywhere, people were murmuring and crying. Someone was gagging in the corner. Loved ones whispered prayers and magazine pages were turned. She clawed at the collar of her shirt. She needed space. The mix of antiseptic, vomit, body odor and blood suffocated her. She struggled to draw in air, her breathing becoming rapid and shallow. Her pulse raced, her panic growing with each beat. She drew her knees to her chest and wrapped her arms tightly around them, tremors setting her muscles to quivering. Unblinking, she faced the door Joao had been taken through, too scared to move in case he needed her.

What felt like an eternity later, Luciano charged into the waiting room, demanding to know where his friend had been taken. The receptionist sympathetically informed him there had been no updates, but he was in the best possible care. Frustrated, he raked his fingers through his hair and turned, seeking a place to sit, and spied Gabi.

"Have they told you anything?"

She swallowed. "Nothing," she said, her voice raspy. "I need to call Mae and Papai, but I don't know what to say."

"I called Frankie on my way here. She will tell your parents, and I am sure they will be on the next plane out."

"Luciano?" Gabi said softly.

"Yeah?"

"I'm scared."

He squeezed her hand, his own trembling. "Me too."

～

"IS THERE ANYONE FOR JOAO ROJAS?" A white coat clad doctor stood, scanning the waiting room for a response, clipboard held loosely in one hand.

"Yes!" Gabi waved her hand as she leapt to her feet, Luciano beside her.

"If you would like to come with me, you can see him now," the doctor said, ushering them through what had only recently been an insurmountable barrier. "I'm Doctor Norman. May I ask how you are related to the patient?"

Gabi stepped forward. "I'm Gabi Cabrera, his manager, and I have written consent from him to be able to make any medical decisions on his behalf. Luciano is his friend. Is Joao going to be okay?"

Doctor Norman handed Gabi a sheath of paperwork. "I'm going to need you to fill these in." She nodded compliantly, barely glancing at them, so focused on what the doctor would say next. "I'm not going to sugarcoat it. He's in a very bad way. We will have to do further investigations before we know the full extent, but for now, he is stable. We suspect he has a spinal injury, possibly thoracic and head injuries. The arm, to be blunt is a mess and is going to need extensive surgery and rehab if he has any chance of regaining use of it."

"Can we see him? I bet he's complaining about having to stay in hospital," Gabi said, relief flooding through her at the thought that Joao's injuries were something they could manage. Come up with a treatment plan, schedule, control.

"Miss Cabrera, I'm sorry, maybe I wasn't clear. Although he is stabilized, he is still in the intensive care unit and will be for some time. We have placed him in a medically induced coma until we can be sure that he hasn't done significant injury to his brain."

Gabi went cold at his words, her stricken gaze flying to Luciano's grim face, and then the world went dark.

CHAPTER 12

The welcoming blackness seductively beckoned her to return to its numb embrace. She could hear the beeping of machines and the metallic slide of a curtain being pulled along its rod. Somewhere, Luciano was talking.

"What does this mean for him?"

"His prognosis is a tough one," the doctor admitted. Groggily, Gabi searched for his name. Ah, yes, Doctor Norman. "Head injuries have so many variables that impact outcomes. He could have balance issues, hearing and sight loss, speech problems. We will need to wait until the swelling goes down for the spinal injury. Best case scenario, we can do spinal stabilization surgery and he will need rehab and time in a clam brace. Still, there is a chance he will have mobility issues." Gabi opened her eyes, surprised she was laying on a bed in a hospital ward, the curtain open between her and the occupant of the next bed—Joao.

The doctor glanced down at his notes and sighed heavily. "That's not even going into his arm injury. He has torn ligaments, tendons, muscle. The shoulder was dislocated, and the elbow broken. That alone has the potential to be career ending. Any of these injuries alone are career ending," he amended. "But together?" He shrugged doubtfully.

"Joao is a fighter," Gabi whispered.

Luciano smiled at her. "So you have decided to join us now. Were you jealous of the attention Joao was getting?"

"Something like that." She gingerly sat up, the world spinning briefly before it righted itself on its axis. "So, now we just wait?" she asked the doctor.

"Yes. You are welcome to stay with him, but we ask that only one stays with him at a time as we have other patients in ICU and we need to keep it restful."

Luciano looked intently at her, gauging her reaction. "I think maybe you would like to stay with him?" he asked.

Gabi gazed at Joao's face, peaceful in repose, despite the oxygen tube coming from his mouth. "Yes. I think I need to be here with him."

Luciano nodded in understanding. "You call if anything changes or you need me." He gave her a tight hug and left.

Easing herself off the bed she had been laid out on when she fainted, Gabi tentatively walked over to Joao and pulled a chair closer to him. Mindful of the IV lines, she desperately gripped his hand, trying to put all the strength flowing from her own into his cool, limp one. Closing her eyes, she prayed.

STRETCHING HER ACHING MUSCLES, she gazed at Joao, the image tugging at her resolve to be strong. Stitches had been placed to stem the flow of blood from where his head had made contact with the bull, his eye beneath swollen and purple, the ventilation tube protruding from his mouth. The arm opposite her was swathed in bandages and strapping to keep it immobile, not that there was much chance of him moving. The entire time she had been there, the only motion had been the steady rise and fall of his chest. Something that her eyes were drawn to time and again, as if pulled to reassure her that he was still in there somewhere.

Suddenly, shrill beeps erupted from the monitor Joao was hooked up to, ominously similar to those in the ambulance. Clutching his hand, she wildly looked around for assistance. The alarm spiked her fear that something was deathly wrong. Dropping his hand, she bolted through the curtains, screaming for help, only to be confronted with medical staff pouring into the corridor. She rushed back to the room, fearful that she would be excluded if she remained outside, only just squeezing herself into a corner before a nurse efficiently closed the curtain. The only words that Gabi could make out were blood pressure plummeting, heart rate and, alarmingly, code red. More medical stuff piled into the room and, without a glance in her direction, the sides of his bed were pulled up, the IV attached to the bed frame and, with the brake released, Joao was wheeled out of the room and through foreboding doors.

"No, no, no," Gabi muttered frantically, shaking her head. "Don't you dare do this to me again, Joao Rojas!" Helpless tears welled, her bottom lip quivering. She glanced around and, spying a nurses' station, she hurried over. "Excuse me, where did they just take Joao Rojas?" she asked a tired looking nurse, the fluorescent lighting unkind to her.

"He was the patient that just had the code red?" the nurse asked, her professional tone belying the kind sympathetic look she gave Gabi.

"Yes, I think they mentioned that."

"A code red usually means that an operating room needs to be prepped. But let's see what I have on the computer." Her fingers were quick across the keyboard. "Yes, as I thought, he's been taken to surgery. That's all the information I have for now, I'm sorry. I will have a doctor come and talk to you as soon as someone is free."

Tears slid down Gabi's ashen cheeks. "Um, thank you," her voice cracked.

Calm eyes that had seen human loss and pain many times in her career softened in empathy. "If you like, you can wait in the visitor's lounge. I will make sure you are kept informed."

Gabi nodded, powerless to find words against the hard lump of fear that filled her to the core. Head down, she shuffled off in the direction the nurse had indicated.

IT WAS clear that someone had tried to add warmth to the otherwise sterile visitor's lounge. Generic wall art hung on the white walls, a potted plant in the corner. There were even sofas arranged in little groupings. None of this hid for one second that the room was in a hospital. The emotions of previous occupants were almost tangible, hope battling with fear, dread turning to anguish. If Gabi closed her eyes, she could picture the ghosts.

"Gabriella, my darling. How is he?" Mae opened her arms wide, her face grave.

"Oh, Mae," Gabi cried, flying into her embrace. "I don't know." She sobbed into her mother's shoulder, the fear no longer able to be restrained. "He stopped breathing in the ambulance and then he was fine again. But he hasn't woken up, and then they called a code red and took him away and now I don't know what's happening." The words fell from her mouth, the rawness of her soul exposed.

Senhor Eduardo gathered his daughter and wife in his strong arms. "Joao is strong, he will fight." Gabi nodded, trying to draw strength from his words. "Now we need to be strong for him."

The sound of a throat clearing cause Gabi to raise her tear-stained face. Taylor stood awkwardly in the doorway, her forgotten suitcase beside him and the smell of fresh coffee wafting in. "I'm sorry to interrupt, but I wanted to return your belongings to you before I catch my flight home."

"Thank you," Gabi said, freeing herself from the support of her parents. "That's very kind of you."

He looked down at the steaming cup in his hand and thrust it out at her. "It's the least I could do, considering the circumstances." Gabi gratefully accepted the brew, its warmth welcome against her chilled hands. "How is he?"

"He's in surgery. That's all I know."

Taylor shuffled his feet, avoiding eye contact with her. "We are all praying for him, but, um, in light of recent developments, you understand that Ironside Protection will no longer be taking part in sponsorship negotiations. Because, um, we don't know…" His voice trailed off pitifully.

Gabi was surprised her body could handle any more emotions, rage rocketing through her. "Till we know what? If he will ever walk again? If he is going to be a vegetable?" she burst out furiously, losing her mind at him. "How about if he dies or not?"

Mae wrapped her arm around Gabi, Papai stepping up on her other side. "I think it is time you leave," Senhor Eduardo suggested firmly, his expression unfriendly.

"I get that it isn't personal, just business. But man, your timing is pretty crappy. Really crappy," Gabi said, drained. The rage that flared so brightly moments ago had extinguished.

"If things change, we will be in contact," Taylor offered by way of consolation, shifting his weight, no doubt aware of how patronizing his comment came across.

"Just get out. No matter what happens from here on in, Joao Rojas has no need of anything Ironside has to offer." Head held high, Gabi turned her back on Taylor, listening as his footsteps faded away.

"I am proud of you," Senhor Eduardo said. "Now, save some of that fight for Joao."

CHAPTER 13

He was young in his blue scrubs. That was the first thing that struck Gabi when the doctor entered the room. Surely too young to give them bad news. Hope fluttered in her belly, even as apprehension tried to pull it down and tear its wings off.

"Mr Rojas has come through the surgery well and is now in a stable condition."

"I've heard that a few times in the last day," Gabi contended. "And then he keeps getting worse."

The doctor nodded sympathetically. "With the seriousness of the injuries that Mr Rojas has sustained, it can be difficult. We are confident that we have stabilized him this time. He had a brain bleed and we performed head decompression surgery to relieve the pressure. The blood pressure drop and heart rate difficulties are common symptoms." He glanced down at Joao's patient chart. "Over the coming weeks, he is going to need more surgery on both his spine and arm, but I will let the consulting surgeons undertaking those procedures discuss outcome with you." He smiled, relieved to have come to the end of his spiel. "Do you have any questions?"

Gabi focused intently on his words, taking in every nuance. "How long will he remain unconscious for?"

"We will start lightening the level of sedation in the coming days as we continue to monitor him. All going well, we are hopeful he will regain consciousness in a week."

Gabi nodded, glancing at her parents. "Can we see him now?"

"Of course. If you would like to come with me." They followed him out. Gabi was relieved to be returning to Joao's side, unwilling to admit just what it had cost her to be separated from him.

Sra Ana cast a worried look at her motionless daughter clutching the hand of the fallen cowboy. She had refused to leave for anything longer than a quick bathroom break before rushing back to his side. Under any other circumstance, her daughter's devotion to the ever-faithful Joao would have filled her with happiness and she would have been quick to call her friend, Joao's mother, to start planning the much longed for wedding. But now? All Sra Ana dared pray for was that the Joao they all knew and loved would return whole to them.

"Gabriella," she called softly. "Your papai and I are going to leave for the night. I think it is best that you come with us, have a rest, something to eat."

Gabi raised strained, bloodshot eyes to meet her mother's. "I'm not going anywhere until he wakes up."

Senhor Eduardo gave his daughter a kiss. "You give us a call if anything changes or if you change your mind and want a rest."

Sra Ana took his place once he stepped back, embracing her daughter for a heartbeat before kissing her farewell. "She will not change her mind once it is set. She gets her stubbornness from you."

~

GABI BADE FAREWELL to her parents and resumed her position, gazing at Joao's bandage-swaddled head, gently stroking his hand. "See? I'm not going anywhere, so you need to get better and wake up." She sniffled. "Now you're just being mean. You can't have a fight and then die." She smiled sadly through her tears. "Don't you know I need to have the last word?" Gabi stared intently at Joao, willing him to show the slightest sign he had heard her words. Her throat constricted, a heavy despair settling over her limbs. "If you just wake up, I promise I will listen to whatever you have to say." She sniffed again. "I might even let you buy me a drink." His familiar face blurred. "Oh, Joao." She sobbed, laying her head on the bed, his hand clutched to her cheek, lost to everything but her anguish and the steady beep of the machines reassuring her that somewhere inside, Joao still fought.

~

"HI GABI," Nurse Owen greeted, picking up Joao's chart from the end of the bed. "A big day today."

Gabi smiled brightly, excited at the prospect of Joao coming off the ventilator, a step closer to him coming out of the coma. If she hadn't thought any further than him regaining consciousness and what that might mean for her feelings, then that was something that she didn't care to delve any deeper into.

"How long will it take till we know…?" She left the question hanging.

The older woman reattached the chart to the bed and laid a comforting hand on Gabi's shoulder. "Unfortunately, this is just one of those things that is in the Lord's hands. The signs are all positive. He has good brainwave activity and the bleeding has stopped, but we won't know for certain until he comes around."

Gabi nodded, smoothing the rumpled hospital blanket that covered the slumbering man, a cold sheen of perspiration on her forehead, fearful at the thought that this might be all that she was left with—an empty shell.

"Good, nurse, you are already here." Gabi looked up at the coolly professional voice, startled at how quickly things were moving. "If you are ready, we shall begin," the doctor announced, moving to the other side of the bed and directing the procedure. In an almost alarmingly short period of time, Joao had taken another step in his recovery and was breathing on his own for the first time in several days. "Continue with the monitoring and notify if there are any changes." And just as abruptly as he had arrived, the doctor was gone.

"Now we wait," the nurse said kindly.

"Now we wait," Gabi repeated, reclaiming Joao's hand. But she was no longer sure what to expect at the end of it.

THE MOVEMENT BEGAN SO FAINTLY that, for a moment, Gabi thought it was a product of her wishful imagination. The next twitch was unmistakable, his eyelids beginning to flutter, his eyes clearly moving beneath the lids. She hurriedly pressed the buzzer, holding her breath so as not to jinx anything. The nurse entered just as Joao made a low groan and began to check his vitals.

"This is a good sign," she said, making notes on his chart. "He's starting to come around." And with that, she left, leaving Gabi to continue her vigil.

That afternoon, Joao groggily opened his eyes and Gabi was certain he looked straight at her before muttering incoherently and closing them again. Hope swelled in her heart till she felt giddy with the euphoric feel of it. But that was nothing compared to his next awakening.

"Gabriella." His voice was raspy with disuse, the words slurred, and held a note of wonderment. "My beautiful Gabriella. You stayed?"

"Of course, I did. Joao, you have no idea how glad I am that you are awake," Gabi said, close to tears. "Do you remember anything?"

"My throat is sore. I feel like I am riding on the back of the softest clouds. It is warm, like how I love you," Joao said, staring at her slack-lidded.

Gabi didn't know whether to panic or giggle, hovering between the two emotions, intensely curious as to what he would say next. "They have you on some pretty strong painkillers."

"I think drugs make you more beautiful," he vowed, reaching for her hand. "But my love for you makes my throat sore."

"Gee, thanks." She giggled, lightheaded with relief that, although he wasn't making the most sense, he was still Joao. Well, a euphorically doped-up version.

"Gabi, I need to ask you something very important." He peered at her owlishly, gripping her hand tightly.

"What is it?" she asked, amused at what could come next.

"The plants. Do you think they are farming us?"

"What!?" she spluttered.

"The plants, they farm us, feed us oxygen, so they can eat us when we turn into mulch." His eyes grew heavy again. "I do not like worms."

"No? I guess I have never really thought about it." But Joao was already snoring softly, returned to the gentle arms of slumber. Gabi looked at him, giggling hysterically, the strain of the last week beginning to lift. She didn't know whether to be disturbed by his question or impressed. But one thing was for certain—the man sure had a heck of an imagination.

CHAPTER 14

The final haunting refrains finished as the last credit rolled. Gabi reached for the water jug and filled the glass up. "I think that has to be one of my top three John Wayne films," she announced, adjusting the bendy straw as she brought it to Joao's lips.

Joao took a steady sip, his eyes flashing his disagreement. "*Liberty Valance*? That's not even top three."

"Yes, it is. *Liberty Valance*, *The Searchers* and *Rio Grande*," she countered, ticking them off on her fingers.

"*The Alamo*, *True Grit* and, I agree, *The Searchers*."

"*The Alamo* is more of an ensemble piece," Gabi argued, shaking her head emphatically.

"I did not know this was against the selection category." He gave her a lopsided smile, dark hair peeping out from beneath the bandages. "I think you are still hanging around because you like to have someone to argue with and that someone is me," he stated confidently, weakly laughing at her ornery expression before immediately wincing in pain.

"You're both wrong," Officer Steele interrupted, entering the room. "His best film was *Stagecoach*."

"You only think that because you're old enough to have seen it when it came out at the cinemas," Officer Thompson teased, hot on his heels.

"How old do you think I am?" he asked in astonishment, eyes opened wide in mock offense.

"I think you and Father Time might be the same vintage." Officer Thompson winked at Gabi and Joao, laughing when her victim spluttered in protest.

Gabi beamed at the pair. "Joao, these are the medics who saved your life. The distinguished gentleman is Officer Steele, and the giggling lady is Officer Thompson. If they hadn't got your heart going again, I don't…" Her voice trailed off, choked in tears.

"But we did get it started," Officer Steele said. "Now they just need to get him all patched up. Speaking of which."

A small thin woman wearing blue scrubs entered the room. "I should have known you would be in here causing trouble when I heard all the laughing," she admonished Officer Steele. "You would think, at your age, you would know better than getting the patients all agitated."

"It wasn't me, Doctor Chapman," he protested, his innocence written across his face. He glared at his chortling co-worker. "You're not helping."

"I'm not trying to," was the quick rebuttal.

Gabi laughed, it was delicious to have the constant weight of worry lifted from her shoulders, even if it was only for a lighthearted moment. The doctor approached the bed and scanned the chart. "I am here to have a quick chat before we prep you for your surgery. Do you understand what procedure you are having today?"

"That's our cue to leave," Officer Steele said, hesitantly flicking a wary glance at Doctor Chapman.

"Are you still here?" she replied, not even sparing him a glance.

"No, Doctor." He scuttled from the room.

Officer Thompson shot Doctor Chapman an admiring look before she slipped from the room. "I need to learn how to do that."

The ghost of a smile whispered across the doctor's lips, making her look younger. "I like to keep him on his toes, but I am sure you know what I am talking about," she said, winking at Gabi. For a moment, Gabi was taken aback by the directness of her comment. She sheepishly smiled, glancing at Joao from the corner of her eye. Clearing her throat, Doctor Chapman recaptured their attention. "Do you understand what your procedure is today?"

"I am getting my spine and arm fixed," Joao said.

"We will begin to," corrected Doctor Chapman. "The surgery today is a spinal stabilization procedure. It is the first step in getting you moving and walking again. You will need to wear a clam back brace afterwards and we will begin physical therapy tomorrow. While we have you in the operating theater, we will also clean up the shards of bone around some of the fracture sites and correct some issues you have in there which will involve some plates. You will also need physio for that injury, but it will be a long road to recovery and, I am afraid, several more surgeries."

Gabi looked at Joao, the reality of what he faced suddenly real. The cowboy looked intently at the doctor, his gaze never faltering. "Do you have any questions?"

"No," he replied.

"Excellent," Doctor Chapman said, securing the chart at the base of Joao's bed. "The nurse will be in shortly to finalize your preparations and I will see you in theater."

Gabi sought out Joao's hand, never once looking at him, afraid her fear would show. The solid warmth of his touch chased some of the shadows away, but others still lurked just out of reach.

~

IT WAS good to stretch her legs and not feel like she needed to rush back to Joao. Gabi couldn't understand why she found herself unable to remain away from him for any period of time. It was probably because she was the best one to look after all the scheduling and organizing everything Joao would need in the upcoming weeks and months. Wasn't it really what a good manager would do for their client? She smiled at the nurses behind the ICU station and made her way to the visitor's lounge. A coffee and a change of scenery was just what the doctor ordered. She smiled at her own pun as she dug in her pocket for some change for the vending machine, her hand making contact with her phone just as it started to vibrate.

She answered, holding it to her ear with her shoulder, and continued to fumble to get her coins into the machine. "Hello?" she said, almost entirely focused on getting some candy to go with her longed-for coffee.

"Gabi? Hello, it's Bryce."

"Dang! Why the heck is the slot so small?" Gabi cussed under her breath as she dropped some of her precious coins on the floor. Dropping to her hands and knees, she peered under the machine, praying they would be easy to retrieve. "It looks like down below hasn't been touched in years. It's pretty disgusting."

"I was going to ask how Joao is, but I'm not so sure I want to know now," Bryce said, mirth threaded through his voice.

"Oh, no, that wasn't Joao I was talking about. All I wanted was some candy, and now I've dropped my last coins under the machine and I can't get any." Gabi's voice wavered. "I know it's stupid to get this upset, but I just really want some." She flopped down on the battered sofa, crying miserably.

"Gabi, darlin', please don't cry," Bryce pleaded over the

phone. "I promise I will get you all the candy you want if you just stop crying."

Gabi hiccupped, embarrassed by her outburst, but unable to stem the flow of tears now they had started. "I'll try, Bryce. Um, but I guess you want to know about Joao?"

"He is the reason I called. But I want to make sure you're okay first?"

"I think all the stress and worry has gotten to me is all. I'm just making a big deal out of nothing and it doesn't help that Mae and Papai flew out yesterday. Joao has gone in for surgery on his back and arm. Lots of rehab and more surgery for the arm. The good news is it appears he is out of the woods for his head injury. I think he is looking at a long hard road to recovery," she admitted softly. "I understand if you want to cancel his sponsorship."

"Hardly. Joao is part of the Black Angus family and we don't turn on family in need. Luciano has been keeping me updated on how Joao is, and the reason I didn't call straight away is I thought y'all might have bigger things to worry about. The other thing I wanted to talk about is that I don't want Joao stressed about medical bills. Black Angus will cover all of it and anything he needs for his recovery—rehab, anything."

Gabi cried harder, her incoherent words jumbling over themselves. In the end, all she could clearly say was, "Thank you."

"I didn't want to make you cry," he said. "Please don't cry."

"What do you expect for being such a nice guy?" she blubbered, blowing into a tissue. "It's your fault."

"All this crying is enough to drive a man to drink. In fact, that's a very good idea. Arrange to send all the medical bills to me and whatever else is needed." He cleared his throat. "Make sure you look after yourself too, Gabi. You are just as important as Joao is."

Long after he had hung up the phone, Gabi sat in the cold, depressing visitor's lounge, nursing a now cold cup of coffee. One single phone call was all it had taken to wash away the sour taste left by her dealings with Ironside. The difference between them was night and day. Although there were very few businessmen that could compete with Bryce, he was and always would be a gentleman cowboy first.

CHAPTER 15

ICU had become comforting, its embrace almost claustrophobically familiar. After two serious incidents that had seriously had Gabi doubting if Joao would live, the reassurance of the constant monitoring had become welcome. But all good things must come to an end and it really was a red-letter day. After several surgeries, Joao was at long last being admitted to the general ward—the last stop at the hospital train line before the home station. Gabi wasn't sure if it was the ambience of ICU or, as she highly suspected, the drugs, but Joao had seemed calmer, more tranquil in there. Now, all bets were off.

"How about we play cards?" she suggested, holding a pack out. "You know you want to." She wiggled her eyebrows comically.

"I am sick of playing cards." Joao glared at her. "And before you suggest it, I am sick of playing games, too."

"I thought you like playing games with me?" she teased, unable to help the flirtation. Silently, she scolded herself for the slip. After all, she didn't like him, did she?

"I am not in the mood, Gabriella." If possible, his jaw jutted out more.

"How about a nice little nap?" she asked soothingly. She fussed with his pillow, his breath warm on her arm. Suddenly conscious of how close she was to him and feeling flustered, she quickly sat back down.

"I'm not five."

"Even big, tough cowboys need sleep."

"I do not need any more sleep. Have you seen this face? It's beautiful. If I get any more sleep, I will be gorgeous." Joao smiled sheepishly. "I am sorry, I want to go home, and I feel like that is never going to happen." He looked off into the middle distance sadly.

Gabi's heart squeezed painfully. She carefully weighed her words. "All we know is what the doctor told us, and he was very honest. Here's what we do know, you are alive." She stressed the last word. "They expect your condition will improve and rehab is going to help with that. This is the best place for it all to happen." An encouraging smile lit her face. "Sure, there's a lot of stuff that we don't know right now. We don't know how much mobility you will regain or if you will ride bulls again." She grabbed his hand, holding it tightly, willing all her confidence in him to flow through it. "But I do know you, Joao Rojas, and I know you will beat this." Her voice rang with conviction.

He gave her hand a gentle squeeze back. "I guess I will have to try. Otherwise, my manager will keep nagging me till I do."

"Seems to me like your manager knows what they are talking about."

"Maybe," he said his eyelids drooping, voice drowsy. "Maybe."

Gabi watched as he faded off to sleep, his grip slackening until it loosened completely. She gently placed it by his side, darting a guilty look to his other injured arm. She pulled a blanket from underneath his bed and spread it out over her lap, settling back to watch his breathing deepen. The tension eased from her body, leaving a pleasant feeling of peace as she gazed at Joao. Everything was going to be okay because she wasn't going to allow any other option. Not to her Joao. Her eyes flew open at the unsolicited thought that barged into her brain. She shook her head. The lack of sleep must be making her silly. Through half-closed lids, she contemplated the slumbering man before her until her own breathing matched his and she slipped into sleep.

SHE WAS BEAUTIFUL, but then, she always had been. Even when she was little, covered in dirt, leaves sticking out of her pigtails, her knees skinned. Joao smiled as she made a little snuffling sound in her sleep, her head resting on her shoulder. The image of her leaning in to fluff his pillow forced its way into his mind, the fragrance of her gardenia perfume still on the stiff fabric of the slip. He could breathe it in if he turned his head. The movement itself was a monumental effort, but a supremely rewarding one as the heady aroma filled his nostrils. An overwhelming need to gather her close filled him, to bury his face at the source of the intoxicating scent.

Frustration snaked up, sinking its fangs into his soul. A man did not lay in bed while the woman he loved awkwardly slept hunched to one side in a chair. He promised himself he would get better and be the man his Gabi deserved, or he would let her go. Closing his eyes against the sharp pang the mere thought of losing her spiked him with, he determinedly focused on flexing his toes. He winced, concentrating on each muscle as it strained and stretched. He would not lose her.

~

"So, when are you coming home?" Frankie asked, her voice echoing over the phone.

Gabi could picture her friend sitting at the table in the gooseneck trailer, fussing with whatever was in front of her as she spoke. "Are you missing me?"

"Of course. But seriously, you have been gone for over a month now. I mean, we are all managing. I'm doing good on the road, and Deb and Megan have everything back home covered. We're just all wondering when you will be back?"

Gabi pondered her words. "Um, well, Joao is progressing well. In fact, he is doing a physical therapy session right now."

"It's so good to hear he is going well, but I think we all understand that it's going to be a long road to recovery for him. How long are you planning on staying there?" A sudden sharp intake of breath came from the other end of the line. "You're planning on staying there till he's discharged, aren't you?"

Gabi glared at her arch nemesis, the candy vending machine. Dear Lord, she needed some sugar. "For now, I need to focus on him. And as you said, you guys have everything under control."

"Oh my gosh, I am so happy for you guys," Frankie squealed through the phone. "Just wait till I tell the others."

Gabi was at a loss for words, her brows drawn together in confusion. "Um, tell them what?" she asked slowly.

"That, you know, you and Joao."

"Me and Joao, what? There isn't a me and Joao." Gabi denied vehemently, wondering what on earth her friend was going on about. "I'm here because Joao is my client and I am doing what any good manager would do in these circumstances." She pulled the phone away from her ear as peals of laughter exploded down the phone line.

"Good one," Frankie chuckled, finally calming down enough to be coherent. "Like you would spend months in hospital for Luciano or me."

"Well, this is different." Gabi folded one arm across her chest, dolefully eyeing the candy. "If you got hurt, Luciano would be here for you and vice versa. I am all that Joao has." The rightness of the words struck her hard, leaving her silent. An opportunity that Frankie was not going to miss.

"Yes, you are all that Joao has ever wanted. Gabi, I love you, but I need to say this as your friend. It's time to be honest with yourself, even if you won't be with us. You care about him, and after you almost lost him, maybe you should be honest with him too."

A strange feeling stretched through Gabi's entire body, overwhelming and yet a sense of completeness, absolute. Dangerous and yet safe at the same time, her heart dancing around her chest, constricting. She shook her head at the silliness of it all. She couldn't possibly have feelings for Joao, he was just a friend she had been worried about, that's all. Honestly, she didn't know why everyone kept going on about it.

She was still shaking her head as she made her way back to Joao's room to await his return from therapy. A large cardboard box sat on his bed. Perplexed, she tilted her head to one side, curiously peering at it. Stepping closer, she was surprised to see her name listed as the receiver. Glancing around and seeing no further information, she carefully opened the package. Inside, nestled safely on packing bags, was a kaleidoscope of candy, for all the world looking like someone had robbed Willy Wonka. Gabi picked up the little card sticking out.

I hope this will get you through your hour of need.
Let me know if you need more.
Always there in a crisis.
Bryce

"Thank you, Bryce," she cried, falling upon the sugary treats, ravenously tearing at the wrapping before stuffing piece after piece into her mouth. She paused and momentarily considered if this act was enough to supplant Frankie as her best friend. Maybe she should put Frankie on notice, she decided before stuffing another piece of candy into her mouth. After all, it was the least she could do after the awesomeness Bryce had sent her way.

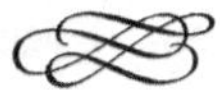

CHAPTER 16

It was impossible not to gape at the opulence that surrounded her. Every available surface gleamed, the timber varnished to such a sheen that Gabi could see her face reflected back at her. "How rich is this man?" she muttered under her breath.

"I'm sorry, miss. I didn't quite catch that." The sleekly coiffured hostess held a beverage out for her.

"It was nothing. Have you worked for Bryce long?" Gabi asked, striving to appear as if flying on a private luxury gulfstream aircraft was a usual occurrence for her. When Bryce had offered the use of his plane to get Joao home, her only thought had been of his comfort. The luxurious reality was something else.

"I have worked as a steward for Mr Dougson since he purchased this plane two years ago." The hostess smiled the bright, false, uninterested smile that came from experience of dealing with egos in the air. "Is there anything else I can get?"

"No, thank you. I should be checking on my friend," Gabi said, unbuckling her seatbelt.

"Of course, if you would like to follow me."

Gabi frowned at her. It wasn't like the plane was so big she couldn't find him, especially since, with the exception of the hostess, pilot and co-pilot, she and Joao were the only people on board. "Of course," she agreed, biting her tongue and following the other woman to the rear of the plane. She had been eager enough to accept Bryce's offer just for the extra space and comfort it would give Joao, but her amazement and gratitude had known no bounds once she had discovered the aircraft contained a bed. With the aid of the medical transport staff, she had been able to get him secured in the bed where she now found him watching the TV at the foot of it.

"Gabi, remind me to thank Bryce when I see him next. This plane even has sports channels." He closed his eyes, breathing in deeply with satisfaction. "A man could get used to this kind of lifestyle. How much do you think one of these would cost?"

She looked around, appraising the wealth on display. "At a guess, an easy forty million dollars." She broke eye contact and shrugged. "Maybe more." Gabi sat down on the sofa opposite him, tucking her hands behind her elbows.

He turned his head to look at her from where he lay on his back. "So, in a few hours we will be home." Gabi nodded, tucking a stray strand of hair behind her ear, still not meeting his eyes. "Gabi, it is okay if you have changed your mind. It is a lot to ask of you."

How to answer that question? When it had been discussed in hospital about care arrangements for when he was released, it had all seemed so clear-cut. Joao needed someone to stay with him make sure he kept to a rehab schedule and did what he was told and, as his manager, Gabi felt that she was the most qualified. Honestly, it was what was best. But now? Now that it was all happening, that very soon, for the unforeseeable future, she would be sharing a house with Joao, it was all a bit daunting really.

She looked up, struck by the intensity of his expression, his liquid eyes scrutinizing her. She smiled awkwardly, unsure of what he was thinking. "Joao, I'm not having second thoughts. There was no way they were going to let you out if you were going to be by yourself. Anyway, it's in my best interest, as your manager, for you to get better so that I can start charging you a fee again."

Those inscrutable dark eyes stared at her, as if seeking a way to see straight into her heart. "Ahh, well, no one can say you are not a committed manager." He blinked, breaking the contact. "I have been thinking about my bed you will be sleeping in."

Her cheeks grew hot. "I, um, don't think you need me to care for you that closely," she babbled. "That's hardly professional."

He laughed delightedly. "You have misunderstood me."

"Well, I think how you worded it encouraged me to misunderstand," she argued hotly, her cheeks still flushed with color, her traitorous heart flip-flopping. "So, what exactly were you trying to say?" Her eyes narrowed dangerously.

"I think this is how I like you the most," Joao said amicably. "I know a lot of people who would fear you looking at them like that. But I always think you get this angry with me because you love me." His gaze flickered across her face, daring her to disagree.

"Joao Rojas, I do not like you, let alone love you."

"I think you like me a little," he taunted, his full lips smirking as he enjoyed her passion. A passion that was directed solely at him. "Why else would you have not left my side for nearly two months?" He raised his eyebrows in a challenge. "And I don't believe your excuse that it's only because you're my manager for one second."

"Whatever. You were talking about where I was going to be sleeping and I have news for you—it won't be in your bed." Gabi pressed her lips in a narrow, intimidating line.

"The spare bedroom has a bed in it, but I do not have anything for you to actually sleep on—pillows, blankets. That was what I was thinking about."

She shook her head. Talk about not what she was expecting at all. "That's okay, I can bring what I need over, and I'll set up my computer at the kitchen table if that is all right?"

Joao considered. "No, I do not like that idea. You will need space to be able to do your work and I think you will be uncomfortable working there. There is another spare bedroom. It does not have any furniture, but if you want, I can buy some, and you can set up a temporary office."

Gabi's expression brightened. "That sounds good. It seems like ages since I have been able to get some work done in peace and quiet." She immediately regretted her words as Joao's face clouded, shadowed by guilt. She reached out to touch his arm, unsure of if she did it because he needed the reassurance or her. "I didn't mean it like that. Even at the bunkhouse, I work from the kitchen table with Megan, Mitch, Deb, Grace and even Chloe, when she is there, distracting me." She laughed. "Don't even get me started on when Frankie is in town. She destroys any organization I have. The girl is a walking natural disaster."

His jet-black eyes unreadable, he nodded. "It's settled, then."

～

GABI NIBBLED on her nail as she contemplated the room she had spent the better part of the day organizing. The curtains had been freshly laundered and rehung, no longer musty with age. Her belongings had been unpacked into the dresser that was no longer covered in dust. The bed was a sumptuous feast for the eyes with crisp linen whites complemented by velvet pastel pink as cushions of all sizes were artfully arranged against the whitewashed headboard. A textured dusty pink silk duvet promised the beholder a simply divine respite if they only succumbed and lay down. A chunky white knit blanket lay draped across the foot of the bed.

Gabi gave a contented little sigh. It wasn't perfect. She still needed to shop for furniture for the office tomorrow, but it was a start. *I'm going to be very happy here.* The thought caught her off guard. *I will make the best of the situation*, she corrected her errant consciousness.

"Bloody hell," Deb said carrying a box. "Made yourself right at home, haven't you?"

"You would want some comfort too if you had just spent the last couple months propped up in a chair," Gabi retorted, uncomfortably aware that her friend's comment mirrored her own earlier thought.

"Where do you want these boxes?" Megan asked, Frankie close on her heels.

"Just in the room next door. I haven't set up the office yet." Gabi showed the girls the way.

"I call dibs on Gabi's room now that she's moved out," Megan said.

"That's not fair," Deb grumbled. "It's the biggest room. If anyone should get it, it should be me and Mitch."

"No one is getting my room because I haven't moved out," Gabi said, exasperated.

"You could have bloody fooled me," Megan muttered,

adding her box to the pile. "I wouldn't be surprised if our kitchen sink isn't packed in one of these boxes."

Gabi groaned theatrically, her hands firmly on her hips. "Go ahead. Get it all out of your systems," she encouraged. Megan's eyes guiltily darted to Deb, who returned her look with a shrug, innocence shining from her face. Frankie gave a guilty cough that suspiciously sounded like a smothered laugh.

Gabi waited patiently, her brows raised. "Nothing? I must say, I am a little disappointed. I was expecting a lot more teasing." She speared Deb with a level look. "Especially you. But if that's all you guys have, I suggest you get a wiggle on and get the rest of those boxes."

SHIFTING his grip from the walker to the armrest of his wheelchair, Joao transitioned his weight until he could lower himself down. Agitatedly, he could feel Carlos's pitying stare as he completed the task. Joao knew Gabi would have kept Carlos updated on his condition. She always raved about how he made progress every day, but to be honest, he didn't feel like it. He was just a has-been, a once strong, fit cowboy who was now reduced to feeling like he had run a marathon after even the simplest tasks.

"I guess I should congratulate you," Carlos said in a light-hearted tone as he raised his glass. "It appears you have accomplished something that I, for one, doubted you ever would."

Joao threw him a questioning look, his chest still rising and falling rapidly as he caught his breath. "I am not sure I even want to know what you are talking about."

"You managed to get my sister all to yourself."

Joao smiled, his eyes soft and content. "She has her own

room, and it is only temporary." His smiled broadened. "But based on the number of things she has deemed necessary for her stay, I am not so sure."

"Yeah, Gabi is not exactly renowned for traveling light. She likes her creature comforts." Carlos chuckled. "The universe must have a really perverse sense of humor. All those years of dreaming what it would be like to have her living under the same roof as you, you finally manage it. And the irony is you aren't in a state to do anything about it."

Joao glared at him, a look betrayed by the twitching of his lips. "You may laugh now, my friend. But you will not be laughing when I ask you to be my best man."

CHAPTER 17

Gabi could see Joao was in intense pain, his usually swarthy complexion now ashen. Eyes closed, he grimaced, taking himself into a deeper place to cope. All Gabi could do was continue the stretch while her heart broke seeing him like that. She hoped all the agony would be worth it.

"I know this hurts, but you have to trust the doctors. They said if we keep doing this exercise between visits, you will see the benefit."

He grunted in response, still unable to formulate words, the torment of rehab having robbed him of the power of speech. Slowly, his harsh breathing eased, and he caught Gabi's hand, holding it to his chest. "I am sorry, Gabi," he said softly.

"What on earth have you got to be sorry for?" Gabi asked, conscious of the steady beat of his heart against her hand.

"That you have to be here doing this." His eyes caught and held hers. "That I got hurt."

"You're being silly. Everyone knows that if you are a bull rider, it's not if you get hurt, it's when. It just turns out you're one heck of an overachiever when you do get injured." She tried to sound flippant, but failed. His eyes bored into hers. "Joao Rojas, how long have you known me?"

"I cannot remember a time that I did not know you, Gabriella," he replied solemnly. "It was as if I came into this life with you held fast in my heart."

The room suddenly grew warm, or maybe it was the color that rose brightly into Gabi's cheeks under Joao's constant regard. She swallowed. "Well then, you would know that I never do anything I don't want to do. I'm here, Joao, because I want to be"—she tapped him on the chest—"and don't you ever forget that." She rose to her feet somewhat stiffly and positioned Joao's wheelchair. After aiding him into it, she pushed her hair from her sweaty face. "I'm going to make both of us a protein shake with extra goodies, and then get some work done." She rested her hand on his shoulder. "That is, unless you need me for anything else?"

"I have kept you from your work too long as it is." His smile did not quite reach his eyes. Those same eyes sadly followed her as she left the room.

Joao held onto Carlos's shoulders as the man's arms wrapped around his waist and lifted him onto the flatbed of the trailer, grunting with effort. "Geeze man, you need to stop letting my sister fill up your plate so much." Above, the sun beat down, pounding on the land where rows of bales waited to be collected. "If I didn't know better, I would say you were taking advantage of this injury to get out of the hay harvest."

"That sounds more like you," Joao retorted.

"Doesn't it?" added Gabi, joining them. "I still remember Carlos hiding down in the hay loft when we were ten or so."

"Wasn't that the time you were hiding for so long you fell asleep?" Joao laughed at the memory. "Your papai gave you a fair whooping when he found you, too."

Wiping the sweat that already gathered at his brow, he stared, squinting against the brightness of the day. Senhor Eduardo, drove the other tractor, while Luciano and Mitch stacked the hay on the back of the trailer. Frankie and Sra Ana were in the house getting the noonday meal ready.

Deb bustled out with Megan, making their way over swiftly. "Sorry, I just needed to get Gracie settled down for a nap, but that was only after she had begged a meat pie and then a sausage roll from Frankie."

Joao smiled at her reassuringly. "You do not need to apologize, I appreciate you—everyone," he corrected himself. "Coming out and helping get the hay in." He looked down at his legs, sharp awareness spiking through him that today, everyone would be putting in more effort than him at his own ranch. Shame flooded him. This wasn't right.

That sense of worthlessness stayed with him throughout the long, dry, dusty, itchy day. A day that, although he donned leather gloves, not once did he employ them. Too useless to work his own ranch. Each time it looked like he might reach for something, one of his friends would appear by his side and take over. A day that, although there was not a whisper of a breeze, swirled with laughter and comradeship.

At the center of it, as with all his life, was Gabi, the beacon that called to him and grounded his very soul. Gabi laughing loudly, her head thrown back at a joke Deb had said. Gabi throwing one of her gloves at her brother, before running away as Carlos chased her down, picking her up and dumping her in the hay. His Gabi that he was forced to watch from a distance, a distance that was beginning to feel insurmountable.

GABI WALKED to where Joao sat watching sports on the TV. Her skin glowed from her shower and she could still smell the fresh scent of her soap. He chuckled as she neared, his focus on her damp hair.

"What?" she asked, her face bright with question.

"You have something in your hair."

She turned a slow circle, trying to peer over her shoulder. "Where?" she asked in laughing defeat, stepping closer to him.

"Only you would be able to wash your hair and still have hay in it." He reached out tenderly to extract the offending pieces of vegetation.

Gabi rolled her eyes. "I know. It's a real life skill." She settled herself down beside him on the sofa. "I don't think there is anything better than having a hot shower after a harvest. It's so nice not to be itchy and covered in dust." She gave a mock scratch.

"When I bought the ranch, I always imagined you working it. But in my version, I was working it with you," he admitted slowly, his gaze creeping up to meet hers. "You are the reason I bought this ranch. I got it because I wanted to prove I could give you what you desired. Then, I could be good enough for Princess Gabriella. When I was a boy, I was so hungry to succeed. Maybe if I just tried hard enough you would see me."

"I don't know what to say." A feeling of heaviness pressed down on Gabi. Guilt for her younger self's behavior and foreboding for what he was to say next.

"Don't say anything, because it doesn't matter anymore. I wanted to prove I could be good enough for you, but fat lot of good it does me now that I'm a cripple. I'm no good to anyone," Joao said in a flat voice, made all the more devastating due to its complete lack of emotion.

"You take that back!" Gabi commanded in alarm.

"Gabriella, I am grateful for all you have done, but I think you should stop wasting your time on me." His eyes dull, he returned to the TV, closing himself off from the conversation.

Gabi slid from the sofa onto the floor, rising on her knees before him, she took his face between gentle hands. Firmly, she forced him to look her in the face. Joao's eyes were frozen, robbed of their usual warmth. He was in there, but it was as if he had just taken a giant step backwards from life. Gabi desperately wanted to reach into him and tell him it wasn't hopeless.

"I refuse to believe that I am wasting my time with you and, one way or another, I am going to make you believe that too."

CHAPTER 18

The warm glow of the desk lamp shone softly on the paperwork scattered over every available inch of Gabi's desk. Pinned to the corkboard behind her was the blueprint for the vet barn, of which building had recently commenced. Post it notes with ideas and to-do lists gave it the scaled appearance of a fish. Invoices and quotes for the build lay neatly in a tray having been checked and actioned, ready to be filed. What drew her attention now was the schedule for the upcoming months for Luciano and Frankie, getting the mix right for competition, promotion commitments and rest.

Rest. Gabi was tired, so drained that even her toenails felt fatigued. But she couldn't let everyone down. The vet barn needed to be perfect, but to get everything she wanted in that build, she needed to watch every penny. And Frankie and Luciano were on fire right now and had a good shot at making the NFR in Vegas. She needed to ensure they had the best chance of making it. Tomorrow, she had to make sure Joao made his appointments with the specialist to see if he required more surgery on his arm. Exhausted, Gabi decided it wouldn't hurt to lay her head down on her desk, just for a moment, to give her tired eyes a break.

~

GABI STOOD, arms folded at the dull thud of muscle hitting the mat. "You almost had it, Joao. Try again," she encouraged, urging him on.

"No, I'm done." He sat up, his bare torso glistening with sweat, ridged with red, angry scars.

Her foot agitatedly tapped the mat, her mouth pressing into a thin line. "The physio said you needed to do this exercise for ten minutes every day. And I think you should listen to what they say, since they've managed to get your butt walking again."

Tired, bloodshot eyes glared mutinously back at her. "Leave it, Gabi. You don't know what you are talking about." Legs trembling with the effort, he picked himself up from the floor, grateful that his balance had not deserted him for the time being.

Fire spat from her eyes. "Oh, so now I don't know what I'm talking about?" The rate of her foot tapping increased. "I think you'll find I know enough to follow instructions from medical professionals." Joao picked up a towel from the bench, wiping his face as he slowly, but determinedly, exited the room. "Joao Rojas, don't you dare leave this room," she hollered at his retreating back. "I never thought you were a coward."

Every muscle quivered with rage. He lashed out, punching the wall. The pain came as a welcome relief. He was used to physical torment by now. "I said leave it, Gabi. I'm not worth it," he roared.

Warm hands gently traced the scars on his back. "You're wrong, Joao." Her voice, so sweet, filled his head. His muscles tensed at the delicate touch of her fingertips. "You are worth it to me." The coolness of air hit his skin as he turned slowly to find himself alone.

~

THE ROOM WAS FILLED with chatter, the clutter of coffee mugs being filled and the lid of the cake container being removed to display its precious cargo of sugary goodness. Gabi breathed deeply, feeling her lungs fully expand for what felt like the first time in months. This was exactly what she needed. Grabbing her share of the bounty, she sat down at her traditional spot at the table. Frankie gave her an understanding look, her tanned face mute evidence to the long hours she had been putting in. Gracie scampered up onto Gabi's lap, helping herself to the cake on her plate.

"Hey, you," she said in laughing protest. "Doesn't your mother feed you?"

Deb rolled her eyes laughing. "That's all it bloody seems like I am doing lately. I can give her breakfast here and then she goes to your parents and has another full breakfast again."

Frankie chucked Grace under the chin. "She can't help it. She's just a growing girl."

"Actually, it's worked out brilliantly for us," Megan said around a mouthful of cake, crumbs falling as she spoke. "Sra Ana and Frankie got word that Gracie has been eating a lot and now they keep sending over food parcels. It's been great."

"I bet." Gabi chuckled. "I wonder how I get enrolled in this food delivery service."

"Cute," the toddler on her lap mumbled.

Gabi's face scrunched up. "Did she just say cute?"

"Yeah, it's because your father says that she can have anything she wants because she's cute," Deb said in disgust.

"Sounds about right," Gabi replied, looking down at the little girl. "And he's right. You are very cute."

"So, how are things?" Frankie asked, reaching for her cup.

"The vet barn is right on schedule. Carlos says all the mares are carrying well and Nova is hitting all her milestones." Gabi paused to draw breath. "I have yours and Luciano's schedule leading up to Vegas all locked in. Chloe arrives today for good, and Joao is being an arse."

"He's still improving, right?" asked Megan. "I mean he's started walking unaided a bit?"

"He is improving. But I don't think as well or as quickly as he would want. He's in a really dark place right now and I honestly don't know what to do," she admitted, staring down at her coffee in defeat.

Deb placed a hand over hers. "Take it from someone who has been there. It's like you don't feel like you deserve to even be here. You push everyone away because you're hurting so bad. But don't let him. He needs you."

Gabi blinked back the tears that threatened at hearing Deb's words. "I'm so sorry you had to go through that, Deb."

"Don't be. It was part of my journey, I guess. I was just bloody lucky that all my friends are so bloody stubborn they wouldn't take the hint when I told them to go away." Deb looked around the table fondly. "I bloody love you guys."

THE CHAIN RATTLED as the punching bag swayed, settling into place. Luciano stepped back and admired his handiwork. "I think that should hold in place."

"I take it Frankie talked to you?" Joao enquired darkly.

Luciano sat beside his friend on the bench. "Yes. I wish you had come to me when the anger started to get too much."

Joao looked down at the scabs crusting over his bruised knuckles, mute evidence of his frustration. His thoughts drifted back to that evening a week ago, when he'd found Gabi asleep at her desk, cheek nestled against her folded arms, snoring softly. The guilt had spliced through him, cutting to the core. She was so darn tired, and he was to blame. Her being here with him, looking after everything, it was too much for her. And as much as he wanted to, he couldn't even pick her up and carry her to bed. What did that make him?

"I didn't want to be any more of a burden to everyone than I already am."

"You are like my brother. Carlos thinks of you as a brother. Sra Ana, Senhor Eduardo, to them you are like a son. Gabi—"

"Gabi!" hissed Joao, interrupting Luciano. "I am ruining her life. She hardly sleeps anymore. Did you know that?" Before Luciano could answer, Joao angrily rushed on. "And do you know why?"

"I am going to assume you will tell me," Luciano said good-naturedly.

"Because she spends all her time taking care of me and then, once that is done, at the end of the day, when she has tucked me into bed after making sure I have eaten, she goes and does everything she used to spend all day doing." Joao raked his hand through his ebony hair, the scar on his arm prominent. "And for what? For a cripple?" His voice broke.

"She is doing it because she cares." Luciano's eyes were sympathetic.

"Before this, she was always telling me she didn't like me. How long will it be before she hates me?"

"Gabi is smart, savvy. She knows the worth of what is

before her." Luciano stood, and walked over to hold the bag. "And my little friend here"—he rocked the punching bag, setting the chain to rattling—"is going to make sure you don't damage any more walls."

$\mathcal{D}$oubt pummeled him, mocking his ambitious plan, seeking to cripple him as surely has his body once had. Joao stared stoically out over the dusty practice arena, deaf to the noise of bulls being moved into the chutes.

"And you're sure you have the doc's okay to be doing this?" asked Travis yet again. "And Gabi knows? Because honestly, I'm more scared of her than a doctor."

Joao turned flat eyes to Travis. "I have medical clearance."

Travis didn't press the issue that he hadn't said anything about Gabi's approval. "Well, I guess as long as you are cleared. Especially with everything Frankie and Gabi have done for Teeny. I thought it was real swell of Chloe to send pictures of the foal to Teeny and then she has kept in touch the whole time she was home in Australia. I swear Teeny is chomping at the bit to catch up with Chloe now she's back." The slide of metal on metal rang out as he slid the gate home, trapping the bull in the chute. "This is Marshmallow. He's one of my junior bulls. I thought he might be the best one to start with."

The Brazilian looked down at the spotted bull, his blunt-ended horns rattling the rails. The rapid tattoo of his heart drowned out the rising nausea. Travis efficiently set about securing the rope and buck strap. Checking he had secured everything to his satisfaction, he looked across to the blank-faced cowboy.

"You sure you want to do this? Ain't a man alive who would hold it against you if you wanted to wait a mite longer."

Joao grimly gritted his teeth. "I am ready."

He climbed onto the top of the rail, ready to swing his leg over. Beneath him, the bull began to move restlessly, sensing what was to come, setting the panels to shaking. Joao froze, his muscles locked in place, no longer responding to the messages his frantic brain sent. Shakily, he wiped the back of a clammy hand across his quivering chin, heart now racing painfully fast, black spots dancing before his eyes.

Wordlessly, Travis released Marshmallow from the chute. The bull bucked across the sand before settling, staring out through the rails. Joao jumped as the stock contractor clapped him firmly on the shoulder in silent support. Joao bowed his head low, his gaze downward, attempting to hide his burning eyes. Humiliation scalded hotly through him.

"Maybe your body is ready but your heart is not there yet," Travis said. Joao raised his face, both men looking across at the now peaceful bovine. "And take it from someone who knows. Hearts are tricky things."

Thud, Thud, Bang. Thud, Thud, Thud, Bang, Bang. All against the background of a rattling chain. Gabi smiled at the sight of a shirtless Joao, his scarred torso gleaming with sweat as he pounded the leather punching bag. These days, she marveled at how much progress Joao had made in the long months since his accident. Although not completely back to his pre-accident capabilities, he was nonetheless returning to the formidable physique he had previously possessed.

He is no longer an invalid. A little voice whispered in Gabi's mind. *He doesn't need you here fussing over him anymore.* A cold lump settled in her stomach at the thought of leaving. Anyway, she consoled herself, he still wasn't completely mended.

"You're looking fighting fit," she called encouragingly.

For a moment, when he turned to look at her, his face was that of a stranger, a mask of rage glaring at her. Gabi blinked her eyes, relieved when she opened them to see Joao's familiar gentle features. She offered him a shaky smile. "When I couldn't find you in the house, I knew I would find you here."

He caught the leather bag between gloved hands, stilling its jerking motion. "Do you know why I work out here so much?" he asked her. "It is to get rid of all the rage that I have inside me."

Uneasily remembering his earlier expression, she was still nonetheless quick to disagree. "I don't believe that. You are one of the most gentle, kindest people I know."

"When I was younger, a teenager back in Brazil, I had this anger inside of me all the time and the only thing that made it feel better was to feed it. I used to go out and look for trouble, take on the biggest thug I could find."

"I never knew," Gabi said in a small voice.

"That is because, one day, my papai told me that if I continued as I was, I would end up dead or, at the very least, he would never allow me back to America again." Joao gave a sad little laugh. "You know, it wasn't the dying or not going to America that scared me. It was the fear that I would never see you again."

Gabi yearned to wrap her arms around the hurt little boy

she saw standing before her. "I always thought it was just a little crush, and then I thought maybe you kept at it because you liked teasing me."

"How I feel about you has been the one constant thing in my life—my entire life." Gabi's breath caught at the raw emotion behind that statement. "I could not risk never seeing you again, so I asked my papai to teach me how to get the anger out. So he taught me how to box."

"I sometimes wonder if I need to start doing something like that," Gabi said, trying to turn the mood light. "To hit something after a stressful day."

His beautiful eyes drew her in, a question that she did not know the answer to beseeching her before he turned his head toward the punching bag, considering. "Would you like me to teach you?" Gabi hesitated, unsure. "Scared?" he teased, rattling the bag.

"Never," she said, raising her head defiantly as her feet propelled her forward. "What do I have to do?"

Removing his gloves, he stepped away from the bag and stood behind her, showing her how to make a fist. Gabi looked down at their joined hands, hers appearing delicate against his large ones. She could feel his solid warmth against her back, the musky smell of masculine sweat and something distinctly Joao wrapping around her. Her mouth suddenly dry, Gabi took a step forward, breaking the contact.

"I forgot I need to make a phone call. Maybe you can show me another time." She bolted from the room. She risked a glance backwards and saw Joao put his forehead against the smooth leather of the bag, probably unsure whether to hit it or laugh. But then again, she was fairly certain she always caused a riot of emotions in him, whether she wanted to or not.

CHAPTER 20

The flesh-colored strapping tape contrasted against Joao's skin as he finished strapping his wrist. His body resembled a patchwork quilt in places pale or tanned skin were both crisscrossed with the same piece of tape. His torso, back, ribs, arm, and shoulder were all a richly textured tapestry of tape, scars and flesh.

"I swear I haven't seen this much tape since we did large animal first aid in vet college." Carlos handed a caged face helmet to his friend.

"Joao likes to tell all of the ladies he is a large animal." Luciano gave Joao his Kevlar protection vest. "They are usually disappointed."

"Maybe I am having second thoughts about you guys being here for this." Joao chuckled, side-eyeing both of his friends.

"That hurts," Carlos said, hand on heart. "It really does."

"It's going to hurt a lot more when Gabi finds out," Luciano dryly noted.

"And how is she going to find out?" Joao gave Luciano a level look.

"I have no secrets from my Querida, but I will only tell her if she asks," he solemnly promised.

"I feel so much better now," Joao groaned, eyes heavenward.

~

"HE DID WHAT!?!" Gabi shrieked. "Frankie, put Luciano on the phone right now." She could hear muffled voices before Luciano's voice answered.

"Gabi, it is a beautiful day, no?"

"Cut the crap. Spill," she commanded, her foot beginning to twitch.

He sighed heavily. "I want it on record I withstood all manner of devious torture before Frankie manipulated it out of me."

"He looked guilty and I tickled him until he broke," Frankie yelled in the background.

"Yeah, yeah, you were strong in the face of threats," dismissed Gabi, waving his protests aside. "Luciano Navarro, you tell me this instant."

"You would have been very proud of him, Gabi. He mastered his fears."

"No, Luciano. I would have been proud of him if he had shown a speck of sense and stayed away from the bull completely," Gabi said, her voice rising sharply in volume.

"He is a bull rider. His father was a bull rider. His friends are bull riders. No matter what you want, it is who he is, it is in his blood. You can no sooner ask him to change than for him to ask you to give away your horses."

Gabi had no comeback, but she wasn't done yet. Not by a long shot.

~

"You better not have done what I was just told you did," Gabi threatened, her hand firmly planted on her hips.

Joao looked up from where he sat on the weights bench. "Depends on what was said?" he hedged. "If it was Luciano, he is a known liar. I do not know why I am still friends with a man like that."

Gabi cocked an unamused eyebrow at him, her gaze unblinking. "So, it's true then. You rode a bull?"

"Yes. It was actually the second time I tried, but last time, my nerve broke," he admitted, his voice downcast. "This time, it held strong." Pride laced through his voice.

"And this is the thanks I get for everything I have done for you," she accused melodramatically. "Are you trying to kill yourself?"

"No, but it was something I had to do, and I am not going to stop."

Gabi gave him a hard look. Admitting defeat, she sat heavily down beside him. "How did you feel?"

"Better than the last time I tried," he admitted with a lopsided smile. "And definitely better than the time before that."

Gabi laughed. "I bet. It went well, then?"

Joao stared down at his hands, his fingers laced together. "I think maybe I am a little worried. It did not feel right. I was second-guessing myself."

She reached out and laid her hand on his thigh, her heart heavy. She knew nothing she could say would change his mind, that what he needed from her wasn't a lecture, but support. "This moment you are going through is between you and your body. Your body is well. You are ready. You are Joao Rojas. You have to look inside yourself and see who you really are."

She trailed her fingers up his arm, her brows knitted as if she saw Joao with new eyes, ones that weren't shaded by the dullness of long familiarity. She could see the pulse in Joao's neck rapidly beating as he turned slightly, facing her fully. His lips, those beautiful full laughing lips, called to her and, no longer willing to fight the pull, Gabi traced his mouth lightly with the tip of her finger. It felt slightly chapped, permanently marked by a lifetime out in the weather.

Gabi didn't want to look up. If she did, she knew she would be at the mercy of his questioning eyes, pleading, begging to know what she was doing. And the simple truth was that Gabi didn't know herself, only that she couldn't leave even if she wanted to. She closed her eyes as she leaned in to meet him. She would worry about it later, but for now, there was nothing else. Just Joao.

$\mathcal{W}$ithout conscious thought, the coffee mug was in Gabi's hand, the first milky sip creeping over her taste buds and down her throat. After only a few minutes, she was bathing in the caffeine kick. Behind her, someone coughed discretely.

"Who are you and what are you doing in this bunkhouse?" Deb asked, strolling out from her bedroom, rubbing the sleep from her eyes.

"Very funny," Gabi said, taking another sip, disheartened that it was already lukewarm. "You might want to be nicer to me. I have an offer you can't refuse."

"That's what Mitch said last night, too. Turns out I bloody could refuse it." Deb chuckled. "He was so disappointed."

"Is he gone already?"

"Nope. He is having a lie-in with Grace. She's been having night terrors and the only thing that will settle her is to climb into bed with us."

"Poor poppet." Gabi drained the last of her coffee with a slight shudder. "Where's everyone else?"

Deb looked at the clock on the wall. "Judging by the time,

Megan will still be out running and Chloe's alarm will be going off anytime soon. Was this visit for something in particular, or was it just to check up to see if we were all out of bed?"

"You know I still live here, right?" Gabi said with a laugh.

Deb's eyes opened wide as she feigned surprise. "Are you sure?"

"Yes, I'm sure." Gabi threw a coaster at her friend. "Anyway, smarty-pants, it looks like I won't be needing my room anytime soon. I thought maybe you might want it?" Gabi found it immensely satisfying to watch Deb's mouth gape open. "Careful, dear. You might catch flies like that."

"Back up the bloody apple cart. So, you're moving in with Joao, like, permanently? You sly dog." Deb's eyes were saucer wide as she spoke.

"I didn't say that, exactly," Gabi said. "But it seems a shame to have my room sitting there empty and, as you said, you guys could use the space."

"Nah, there's more to it than that," Deb insisted, leaning her elbows on the table.

"Joao still needs me," Gabi argued.

"I bet he bloody does too." Deb winked, her chair squeaking against the floorboards as she shifted her weight further forward.

Gabi set her jaw. "Do you want the room or not? If you don't, I'm sure Megan or Chloe will."

"Cool your bloody jets, I didn't say that. Yeah, I'll take the room. But it's not going to stop me from finding out what's going on between the two of you."

Gabi stood to leave, sighing in the face of her friend's bulldog determination. "If it makes you feel better, I don't even know."

∼

THE TICKETS LANDED in front of Gabi, writing side down. She stopped her typing to glance up in annoyance. "What are these?"

Joao scratched his face. "They look like tickets, possibly plane tickets."

Gabi closed her eyes against the urge to give in to her frustration. "Yes, I can see that, but why are they on my desk?

He looked at her innocently. "You should have asked that in the beginning."

"I didn't think I had to." Gabi pursed her lips. "Are you going to tell me what these tickets are for? I don't have anything scheduled for you."

"They are two return tickets to Brazil." Joao drew himself up to his full height. "I have entered Barretos."

"Over my dead body and very possibly yours," Gabi exploded, her chair flying out as she burst to her feet. "How you think this is even remotely a good idea, I don't know."

"Gabi, you knew I would eventually return to competition. This should not be unexpected," he said. Gabi jerked her hand away as he reached for it. Sighing, he raked his fingers through his hair. "Gabriella, I am ready."

"Well, I'm not." Gabi stalked to stand in front of the window, her profile silhouetted. "I almost lost you once. I'm scared the next time might be for good," she whispered, so softly it was as if she spoke to herself.

He gathered her stiff unyielding body into his arms, inhaling her fragrance. "For so long, I have yearned for you and now you need to believe me that I would never do anything to jeopardize it." She felt him smile against the top of her head. "That includes dying. But Gabi, I need to do this for me. Just understand that I can't bear to lose you, to lose this thing that you have given me that makes me feel complete. I love you, Gabriella Cabrera."

Gabi turned in his arms, her eyes shimmering as she

looked up into his beloved face. "Falling in love with you was the easy part. Maybe part of me has always loved you. It's the admitting to myself that it's happened, that's the hard part. You're here, and I'm so glad, even if I'm still trying to hide behind my defenses." She stood on her tiptoes till her lips softly met his, luxuriating in the rush of pure love that filled her. "I love you, Joao. But if you die, I am never speaking to you again."

CHAPTER 22

There was no other way to describe Barretos than simply the greatest spectacle on earth. Loud partying groups gathered on every corner, dancing and trumpeting, only to get louder as the night wore on. The air hummed with a vibrancy that was unexplainable. "Strewth. I'm not sure what I expected, but this is next level." Frankie excitedly swiveled her head from side to side, barely blinking for fear of missing something as the girls wove their way through the crowd, arm in arm. "No wonder you never miss this."

Gabi laughed at her friend's enthusiasm. "For us, it is more than that. When we come back, we always catch up with our friends and family and Papai is famous here. That helps A LOT. It means we can pretty much get into whatever we want."

"I bet you bloody got into a lot over the years."

Gabi tilted her head as her mind drifted back. "Not as much as you think. You know all those friends and family I mention, well, that didn't let me get into much mischief at all."

"I'm so disappointed in you." Frankie laughed. "And now that you have finally let Joao catch you, well you've completely wasted your opportunities."

Gabi blushed. "Well, I thought it was time I cut the poor guy a break. He put the time in and, well, Frankie," she went on in a rush. "Once I figured out I love him, I wasn't going to be stupid enough to let someone else snuffle him up."

"Does it get easier each time you admit it?"

"A little," allowed Gabi, her lips twitching. "I did swallow a lot of pride when Mae and Papai rubbed it in—how many times I said that I didn't like Joao."

"I don't know, when they caught up with Joao's parents, everyone seemed pretty ecstatic. But I guess they did all of their gloating in private." Frankie smirked at Gabi. "If you aren't bloody careful, your wedding will be completely planned down to the date and what underwear you're wearing before we leave."

Gabi's face burned ever brighter. "They might have to wait a bit longer. It took Joao how many years to tell me he loved me? Let alone him getting up the nerve to ask me to marry him."

Frankie looked at her friend's face intently. "I think Joao might surprise you this time."

THE RUSTLE of plastic was the only warning before the bag landed heavily in Joao's lap. "Don't say I never get you anything." Luciano settled himself down on the bench beside his friend.

All around the locker room beneath the stands, cowboys wandered, gossiping and teasing each other, laughter masking the nerves. Periodically, there would be the dull thump of a gear bag hitting the concrete floor, the pine smell of rosin battling against the sharper liniments.

Joao peered into the bag, laughing at the contents. "Man, what did you do? Rob a pharmacy?" he said as he pulled roll after roll of strapping tape out.

Luciano shrugged smugly. "Not quite. I just visited the Black Angus Sports Medicine Team at the last rodeo I was at and mentioned I had a friend who was in the grips of a debilitating strapping tape addiction." He smirked at Joao. "Obviously, they knew it was you straightaway." His face sobered. "How are you feeling?"

"There are nerves, but they are good nerves," Joao replied, wrapping some tape around his wrist. "Tonight, I am ready, maybe the most ready I have ever been."

Luciano nodded at Joao's words. "They are starting to call us." He grasped his fellow bull rider's hand firmly, hauling him to his feet. "Shall we go show these bulls what real cowboys can do?"

Joao slid his arms through his protection vest, leaving it unzipped. His fingers crept up to brush the crucifix that dangled from the shoulder strap, seeking reassurance. For a moment, Gabi's brightly smiling face flashed into his mind, leaving a searing determination in its place. Grabbing his helmet, he strode forward, his leather chaps swishing with each resolute step.

"Let's do this."

THE FIRE SENT sparks dancing into the darkness, the smoke tangoing ever upwards. It was impossible for Gabi to fully block out the rabid sounds of the crowd baying at each competitor in the distant horseshoe-shaped stadium. Her sweaty hands shook as she wiped them on her denim clad thighs, her dry mouth making swallowing impossible. A large dark shadow loomed out from the blackness. Gabi jerked back in fright, her body primed to flee.

"I had not thought you would be hiding all the way back here," her papai said, stepping into the warm orange light of the fire.

"I know, I'm a coward. But every time I close my eyes, all I see is Joao strung up on that bull." Her voice was scratchy as she spoke.

Senhor Eduardo offered her a drink, sitting down beside her companionably. "I always said to your mae that I had the easy job—riding the bulls. It is excruciating to watch your loved one put themselves in the path of danger. Most normal people spend their whole lives trying to avoid it." He shrugged, a sheepish smile dancing across his lips. "And then you have bull riders."

"Papai, I love him. I don't know what I'd do if anything happens to him again," Gabi said, her heart in her voice.

"If you love him, you need to love all of him, no matter how hard. No one knows how long we have on this earth, but would it not be better to walk beside him in the light than hiding back here in the shadows?"

Gabi looked fondly at her father. "How did I get so lucky to have such a wise papai?"

"Years of training by your mae." He stood and held out his hand. "Shall we?"

Feeling like a little girl, she let him pull her to her feet. "Yes, Papai, we shall."

Frantically, heart fit to burst from her chest, Gabi wove and ducked through the crowd, her breath rasping as she struggled to suck in oxygen. Long since separated from her papai, her sole focus was to make her way to her cowboy. A blur of lights and shocked faces flashed past her as she sprinted. She barely broke stride as she waved her pass at the security, his eyes wide in his stunned face. Her boots pounded on the concrete, every muscle straining to get to the rails of the chutes.

Cowboys, so many dang cowboys in the way and slowing her down, but with each step, the light was getting brighter, the commentator's voice clearer. She pushed onwards. Across a sea of cowboy hats, she could see Luciano, disappearing as he bent down and then reappeared. Beside him, in the chute, was the movement of Joao's hat. A wall of humanity pressed together, making it impossible for Gabi to continue her forward progress. Defeated, she choked back a frustrated sob as she glimpsed Joao's head jerk as the bull left the gate. Hyperventilating with panic, she whimpered, fearful.

Somehow, as if he could sense her there, Luciano turned his head, his face lighting up as he saw her. He began to urgently call her name and, like a miracle, the crowd of cowboys parted as surely as the Red Sea. But Gabi's legs no longer had the strength to propel her forward. Gentle hands supported her, guiding her onwards. Papai, breathing heavily with his exertions from his own mad dash, was there.

Luciano reached for her arm, her eyes, dreading what they would find, looked to the sand. A riderless bull, its bucking hindquarters blocking her view of the rider, sent her spiraling over the edge, descending her into a blind panic. And then it happened. The buzzer triumphantly rang out over the stadium. Gabi's tear-filled eyes widened as the bull moved off toward the exit chute to reveal Joao punching the air in triumph.

Her legs sagged underneath her and she would have hit the ground if it were not for her father's steadying hand. "Gabriella, he is okay." Her papai shouted to be heard over the cheers of the crowd.

"He's more than okay," Luciano said, slapping the rails in delight. "That's the best score of the night!"

Joao, his face flushed with triumph, accepted his rope from a rodeo clown and made his way victoriously to where they stood at the rail. His eyes roamed her face before locking with hers, and then he was there, his arms holding her, promising to never let go again, his lips against hers. Buffeted by the rollercoaster of emotions she had been on, tears trickled down Gabi's face. She could taste their saltiness as they mingled with their kiss.

Luciano pounded Joao on the back. "Hey lovers, this will have to wait. They are calling for him to collect his prize."

Joao, smugly satisfied, looked down at Gabi. "I am already collecting my prize, right here."

Gabi blushed hotly under his warm regard. "Shoo, go out there."

He held her gaze for a moment longer but did not release his hold on her. "I would have you come out there and share the moment with me." Before Gabi could formulate a response, he was already leading her out to the sand. Joao only relinquished his hold on her when he accepted the winner's buckle and prize check, returning to wrap an arm around her shoulders as he took the microphone.

"Barretos, like a lot of Brazilian cowboys, has always been a dream for me to win. But over the last year, it was one I had almost given up on. If it was not for the strong, amazing woman that stands beside me—" His voice broke and he buried his face in Gabi's hair for a moment before raising his tear-stained face again. "If it was not for her, it would never have happened. And now I can say that I have won at Barretos!" The crowd went wild, appearing as an undulating sea of faces. Joao patiently waited for them to quieten. "But now, it is time. What you saw here tonight, it was my last ride. I am hanging up my spurs."

Once again, the crowd noisily interrupted, a cacophony of anguished cries and cheers. Gabi looked up, her eyes shimmering, her tears trailing unchecked down her face.

"Bull riding has been the most important thing in my life for the longest time, and now"—he pulled her in closer—"now, I have something that is much more precious to me, too precious for me to risk losing." Gabi gave him a watery smile, her heart painfully overflowing with love for him. "When I was recovering, my focus was to return to the arena because, when it was time, I wanted to retire on my terms. And after tonight, I am doing just that. Thank you, Barretos." He handed the mic back to the commentator.

"I love you," Gabi whispered to him.

"I love you, Gabriella, now and forever."

~

WHEN YOU ARE the winner of the biggest rodeo in Brazil, it can be near on impossible to find a moment of quiet. It said a lot for how much Joao desired solitude, that he had managed to pull it off. Gabi looked at him, admiring his proud stance as the firelight glinted off his Barretos Championship buckle. His gentle, soft eyes gazed lovingly into hers.

"It has been one heck of a night," Gabi said, walking closer to snuggle into his arms.

"It's not over yet," he replied, resting his chin on top of her head. "Although, I cannot say how long it will be before we are discovered and forced to re-join the party."

"Not that I am complaining, but don't you want to celebrate your win with everyone?"

"Soon. But for now, there is something else I would much rather do." Gabi gave a little whimper of disappointment as he moved away. "I meant what I said tonight. I have somehow managed to get you to love me and I will never take that for granted." He went down on one bended knee. "Gabriella Cabrera, will you marry me?"

"I guess I had better. Now that you've retired, you're going to be underfoot an awful lot more and someone has to look after you. Last time I checked, I was the most qualified."

Joao gave a soft laugh. "Gabi, my love, only you would use so many words to say yes and still make it sound like it was your idea." His face grew serious. "I know my body is a bit more broken than before, but my heart is a strong as it ever was, and it is all yours," he solemnly promised.

Gabi snuggled into him, no longer willing to not feel his warm body against hers. "I wouldn't have it any other way."

EPILOGUE

*J*oao stood, hip resting against the door frame as he watched his wife hold the tablet aloft. "I think the look I want is ranch meets industrial, with maybe a pinch of Hamptons. I loved what you did at Black Angus HQ, I just want more whites and navies. Do you think you can have some mood boards outlining your ideas to me by next week?"

"I think I have a few ideas that you are going to like," a woman's voice answered through the speaker. "I can't wait to embark on this project. I think it's going to prove to be very interesting. If that's everything, I'm going to wrap this call up and get started."

Gabi pursed her lips with concentration, a look Joao knew all too well. It meant that, somewhere in that pretty head of hers, she was going through a checklist. She smiled. "No, I think that's everything for today, Jade. Thank you." Gabi gave a contented little sigh as she hung up the device.

"The office redecorating is going well, Sra Rojas?" Joao asked, pushing himself off the doorway to enter the room fully.

"Exceptionally well. That woman is a genius. I'm so grateful Bryce shared his interior designer's details."

"I think maybe I will need to get her to help decorate my office, too."

Gabi ceased her perusal of swatches to look at her husband in confusion. "But you can just share mine."

Joao laughed, taking his wife in his arms. It was impossible to be this close and not touch her. "I know how territorial you get about these things. Anyway, I will need more space than you are willing to allocate me."

Gabi stepped out of his embrace, eyes narrowed suspiciously. "For running the ranch?"

He nodded. "For some of the time, yes. But I will also need somewhere to work from as the Manager of Black Angus Sports Medicine Team."

"What?!" Gabi exclaimed, a bemused smile flitting across her face.

"Bryce has asked me to head up their Sports Medicine Team, making sure they have all the funding and everything they need. And also to think of ways to improve the services they provide."

Gabi threw herself into his arms. "How long have you known?" She shook her head. "Actually, don't answer that, it doesn't matter. I can't think of anyone better to do the job." She gave him a lingering kiss. "I'm so proud of you, Joao." She wiggled out of his arms to retrieve her tablet. "Maybe we should brainstorm some ideas, you know, for improvements."

Joao chuckled and gently removed the device from her grip. "There is plenty of time for that later. For now, I would have you close your eyes." Surprising him, she obediently shut them tightly. He walked out into the hallway to collect something and returned. "You can open them now."

"Oh, Joao," she breathed. In his hands was a beautifully carved Affinity Ranch sign. "It's beautiful."

"I had Mitch make it for me. It never felt right to me that Affinity Ranch was tagged on your father's sign. This is where it belongs, just like it is where you belong, front and center."

She gently traced the wording on the sign. "I don't know how I managed to get so lucky."

"I would say it is because I did not take no for an answer," he said, nibbling her lip.

"You know what I'm thinking?" Gabi asked through lowered eyelashes.

"I have a fair idea." He pulled her in closer.

"Do you think we should remove all the fence line between the ranches, or just add gates? There are pros and cons for both ideas."

"Gabi?"

"Yes?"

"Hush and let your husband kiss you." As Gabi surrendered to her husband's wish, she realized that sometimes a cowgirl finds her passion where she least expects it.

THE END

As an Indie Author, reviews help me get my books noticed. If you enjoyed reading Gabi's story as much as I did writing it, please leave a review, it will make all the difference to me.

If you loved, *A Cowgirl's Passion,* sign up for my newsletter at https://www.edithmackenzie-author.com

to get an exclusive prequel, *A Bull rider's Paradise,* Sra Ana and Senhor Eduardo's love story.

Now turn the page as the Affinity Stud Ranch story continues with Megan….

A COWGIRL'S PRIDE SNEAK PEEK

She had been in a lot of places in her life, especially growing up, but never anything like this. The walls still smelled strongly of the paint that had only dried last week, as Megan stepped into the laboratory with the rest of the girls, the aroma from the rubber tiles that covered the aisle and continued into the stalls wafted in after them. Everywhere she cast her gaze was a marvel. The stainless-steel counters still had protective plastic adhered to them, a microscope pride of place on a bench underneath shelving laden with slides, specimen jars and other apparatuses that Megan wasn't familiar with. Swiveling around, she found a sterilization unit, fridge and computer.

"Bloody heck," Deb said in amazed approval. "I can't even process how awesome this all is."

"As the person footing the bill, I can tell you, no expense was spared," Frankie added, smiling with satisfaction at the veterinarian perfection set before her. "But even I am impressed, Gabi."

Gabi graciously nodded, accepting their approval as her

due. "Next on our tour is the mare and foal crush, followed by the operating theater."

"Say what?" Megan asked, unsure if she had heard correctly.

"The mare and foal crush?" Gabi asked, confused about what to clarify.

"No, the other one. Are you saying we actually have a purpose built equine operating theater onsite?"

Gabi smirked. "Yep and the only privately owned one in any barrel racing ranch that I have heard of."

Megan shook her head in amazement. She seriously had to give it to that girl—she dreamed big and usually got her way. *But she's one of those golden people,* the little voice in her head niggled, always finding the negative. *Not like me.*

She waited sullenly while the others trooped from the lab, meaning to join on the end. As she closed the door behind her, she spied a staircase set against one wall. Remembering accommodation was included in the vet barn, she decided to investigate, conscious that this might be her only chance to check it out before Carlos moved in. Her soft footfalls barely made any noise as she traipsed up, the unlocked door only further justifying her decision. The new hinges gave a little squeak of protest as the door smoothly swung open. *Gabi might want to get someone to look at that,* she thought as she peeked in.

Inside, a yellow sofa was barely visible, surrounded by stacks of boxes, a man's shirt carelessly thrown over the top of one. She did a double take. That didn't seem right. Unconsciously, she stepped further into the room as she focused on the garment. The sharp brightness of someone turning the light on made Megan's stomach drop in fright. "What the bloody heck," she uttered in surprise.

"I could say the same thing, but probably not with such an

Australian flavor," a warmly amused, if somewhat sleepy, masculine voice said.

Megan traced the source of the voice to find a shirtless, tousled-haired Carlos lounging against what she could only assume was the bedroom door. "But, no one is meant to be here." She protested, feeling uncomfortably off kilter.

"Well, obviously, I didn't get that memo of Gabi's," he fired back, still looking like he could feature in a hot guys calendar.

"What memo didn't you get?" Gabi's voice said, rising from the stairs. Judging by the sounds, she and the rest of the girls were on their way up.

Frustration left a sour taste in Megan's mouth. *Of course, wasn't it always the way that everyone showed up right when she had made a meal of things? Next, Deb will be making some sort of wisecrack.*

"I see Megan has already sniffed out the hot guy," Deb said entering the room close on the heels of Gabi. "And he doesn't even have a shirt on. Nice work, Megan." She winked at Megan in approval.

"I didn't know he was here," Megan ground out.

"Actually, why are you here?" Gabi asked Carlos, a brow raised suspiciously. "Weren't you meant to be arriving at the end of the month?"

Carlos didn't meet his sister's eyes as he gathered up his earlier discarded shirt. "Well, I tied up loose ends in Kentucky earlier than I expected and I thought I would take the opportunity to start unpacking my things and settle in."

Megan watched his glorious abs vanish from view, covered by his snug-fitting shirt. A quick glance showed that, except for Gabi, everyone else were somewhat saddened by the disappearing act as well.

"What loose ends?" Gabi pushed, undeterred by her brother's dissembling.

"You know, this and that." Carlos scratched his head with a sniff. "I have to give you credit, sis. You did a good job building this. In fact, I was having a top-class nap in the bedroom before the gorgeous Megan interrupted me." He sent her a flirty wink. "She can wake me up anytime."

"For Pete's sake, don't tell her that. You'll never get any sleep again," Deb fired back. Megan shot her a dirty look, promising violence if she didn't keep her mouth shut.

Frankie, intercepting the look, took pity on Megan. "I think we still have a few more things that Gabi needs to show us."

But isn't that always the way, Frankie playing peacekeeper? her mind whispered.

Gabi skewered her brother with a hard look. "Don't think this conversation is over."

"I was never in any doubt. I'm sure you will pick it up at your earliest convenience, which will probably be tomorrow when you corner me as I visit Joao," he replied urbanely.

As everyone left, Carlos called out. "I meant what I said, pretty Megan."

To order Megan's story, *A Cowgirl's Pride,* it is available for purchase on Amazon or free on Kindle Unlimited

ACKNOWLEDGMENTS

A big thank you to Dr Alisa Norman who helped restrained my creative license when it came to the medical scenes, even when she managed to break her wrist whilst on holidays.

A debt of gratitude to my editor Rebekah Groves for her patience with me.

Another big thanks to Megan from Designed with Grace for her cover design. Who knew it was so hard to get pictures of hot cowboys that were wearing shirts.

A cowgirl's movie star

A fiery cowgirl with big dreams. A movie star far from home. When their two worlds collide, will their love be strong enough to hold them together or will they be pulled apart

A cowgirl's billionaire

Release Dec 2020

Christmas Standalone Books

Boots and Mistletoe

ABOUT THE AUTHOR

Edith MacKenzie or Eddie Mac to her friends is an author of sweet and wholesome contemporary cowboy romance. They say in literary circles to write what you know, and Eddie has certainly taken that to heart. Before embarking on a writing career, she trained horses professionally and brings that wealth of knowledge to her writing.

Now a mom to a boy and girl, as well as wife, she delights with her tales of strong cowgirls and their adventures in finding love. When not weaving the love stories of her characters, she enjoys hanging out with her family and animals, as well as reading, fishing and camping

Just remember once a cowgirl, always a cowgirl.

facebook.com/EddieMacAuthor

amazon.com/Edith-MacKenzie

bookbub.com/profile/edith-mackenzie

instagram.com/edith_mackenzie_author

GLOSSARY OF AUSSIE SLANG

Now everyone knows that cobbers from the Land Down Under speak the Queen's English, but if you don't know to Tracky Daks from your Servo, I've put together a quick little cheat sheet.

A few stubbies short of a six pack - Crazy

Ankle Bitter - Small child

Arvo - Afternoon

Blind - Intoxicated

Bloody - Very. Used to extenuate a point

Bloody oath - Yes or its true

Bludger - Someone who is lazy

Buggered - Exhausted

Cark it - Die

Choccy Bikkie - Chocolate cookie

Clucky - Feeling maternal

Crook - Feeling sick

Daks - Trousers e.g. Tracky Daks are tracksuit pants

Dog's breakfast - Messy (does not relate to food), a bit of a
shambles

Dry as a dead dingo's doing - Exceptionally dry

Flat out like a lizard drinking' - Not doing very much at all

Grog - Alcohol

Hit the frog and toad - Hit the road, get going

Man's not a camel - A man gets thirsty and would indeed like
the beverage you are offering him

Mate - Friend or conversely could be someone you
barely know

Nay, Yeah - Yes

Pull the wool over someone's eyes - To trick or mislead
someone

Reckon - For sure

Ripsnorter - Can also be interchanged with beaut, bonza. Someone doing something exceptionally good

Servo - Petrol Station

Six one way, half a dozen the other - Undecided

Sparrow Fart - Before the crack of dawn. Very, very early in the morning

Stone the flamin' crow - An utterance of surprise of annoyance

Struth - God's truth. Used to express surprise or dismay

She'll be right - Everything is going to okay

Tell 'em they're dreaming - Is never in a million years going to happen

Tighter than a fish's bum - Said person is very frugal with their money

To blow smoke up someone's bum - To give praise that might make the other person cocky or overly confident

Up yourself - Stuck up

Ute - Pickup Truck

Whoop whoop - Middle of nowhere

Wrap ya laughing gear 'round that - Eat this

Yarn - To talk or tell tall tales

Yeah, nay - No

You bloody ripper - Very good, a job well done